"What game are you playing now, David?"

"No game. Now what is your experience with men? You've never been married, have you?"

"No, I haven't, and I don't think I ever will be. As for my experience, Doctor, let us say that I very much enjoy reading about a hero who can not only enjoy himself but also the heroine, and vice versa. It's a marvelous fantasy," she added, trying for sarcasm.

David looked at her for a long, thoughtful moment. "I see," he said finally. "But have you ever been in love? Ever wanted a man?"

"No! And tell me, what does 'want' mean in your marvelous lexicon?"

"As in desire, lust after, sigh over—"

"Stop it!"

He grinned at her. "I've got a wager for you, Chelsea."

"The next poker game isn't until next week."

"Not that kind of wager." He paused. "Do you want to hear it?"

Dear Reader,

When two people fall in love, the world is suddenly new and exciting, and it's that same excitement we bring to you in Silhouette Intimate Moments. These are stories with scope, with grandeur. These characters lead the lives we all dream of, and everything they do reflects the wonder of being in love.

Longer and more sensuous than most romances, Silhouette Intimate Moments novels take you away from everyday life and let you share the magic of love. Adventure, glamour, drama, even suspense— these are the passwords that let you into a world where love has a power beyond the ordinary, where the best authors in the field today create stories of love and commitment that will stay with you always.

In coming months look for novels by your favorite authors: Maura Seger, Parris Afton Bonds, Elizabeth Lowell and Erin St. Claire, to name just a few. And whenever you buy books, look for all the Silhouette Intimate Moments, love stories *for* today's women *by* today's women.

Leslie J. Wainger
Senior Editor
Silhouette Books

IMRL-7/85

Catherine Coulter
Afterglow

Silhouette Intimate Moments

Published by Silhouette Books New York

America's Publisher of Contemporary Romance

SILHOUETTE BOOKS
300 East 42nd St., New York, N.Y. 10017

ISBN: 0-373-07190-6

First Silhouette Books printing May 1987

America's Publisher of Contemporary Romance

Printed in the U.S.A.

Books by Catherine Coulter

Silhouette Special Edition
The Aristocrat #331

Silhouette Intimate Moments
Aftershocks #121
Afterglow #190

CATHERINE COULTER

has long been familiar to readers as a best-selling author of historical romances. Recently she began writing contemporary romances, as well, and *Afterglow* is her third entry in that genre. When she is not working on her latest novel, she spends her time sailing, playing the piano or appreciating Mill Valley, California, with her husband, Anton. She also enjoys getting readers' responses to her books and conscientiously answers every letter she receives.

To all my "real" writer friends, who have given me
so many hours of reading enjoyment,
hours of sheer fun in your company.
Not nearly all of you are in the novel,
but I wish you were.

To all my other "real" friends—
Sarah, George, Elliot, Barbara, Beth and Ed.
Life wouldn't be the same without you guys.

Chapter 1

Look, George, I'm not all that *bored*. And what do you do with a man, anyway?" Chelsea broke off abruptly at George's literal belly laugh.

George was eight months' pregnant.

"All right, so Elliot did do something."

"At the very least, *something*," George agreed. "Stop a minute, Chelsea, I've got to move around a bit. The kiddo is growing restless."

Chelsea watched her beautiful friend ease her way to the edge of the chair, shove off using the arms and achieve a less than dignified upright stance. "There! Goodness, another month of this! I'll tell you, Chelsea, I think it would do men some good if they had to go through this." She patted her stomach and began her slow trek around the living room. "I swear the kid's going to be a drummer."

"Have you and Elliot decided what to name it?"

"It? No, whatever it's going to be, it still has no name. I told him if he didn't come up with something soon that I could agree with, I'd leave the state, have the kid and name it Lance or Brigitte."

Chelsea laughed. "Perfect hero and heroine names," she said.

"Come now, Chels, you've never had a Lance in any of your novels, have you?"

"Well, no, not that outrageous. But my Alex and Delaney and Brent, not to mention my Anthony, are alive and well, at least in my imagination."

"Don't forget that medieval hunk Graelam of yours!"

"Wasn't he a marvelous MCP?"

"At least your heroine broke him in the end. And I'll just bet after you got him domesticated on page four hundred and fifty, he became a total bore."

"True enough," Chelsea said, and sighed. "There's not a man around today to compete with his sublime nastiness, but he did live in the thirteenth century, George. He could hardly have been into sensitivity training. Too bad, but we'll never know what happened to his eternal love for his wife after, say, ten years or so."

"They probably both croaked from not bathing," George said.

"Not true. I did have them bathe regularly, and I'll tell you, I felt guilty about it. No more medieval novels for me, except, you know, there was this secondary male character, and my fans seem to like him quite a bit—"

"All right, I've got the picture," George said, grinning down at her friend. "Another macho medieval hero in the works."

"And like Graelam, he'll be great in bed."

"All your heroes are, Chelsea. Now, my dear, let's get back to the present, where men shower and shave every morning. There are good men out there, Chels. I found Elliot, didn't I?"

"He's a throwback," Chelsea said, "to the best of my heroes."

"Oh, come on, Chelsea! Here you are finished with a book and at loose ends for how long—a week?—before you hit the computer grindstone again."

"Yeah," Chelsea agreed. "I sent off an outline for the next one yesterday, and I need to do some historical medical research before I start this one. Tell Elliot the hero is a doctor, and if he's real nice to me, I'll let him provide the raw material."

"He'll love it. Now let's find you a neat guy before you begin total immersion again."

"Where? You know I'm not into singles' bars, George."

George smiled and said somewhat complacently, "Well, as a matter of fact, do you have anything against doctors?"

Chelsea groaned and clutched a sofa pillow over her face. "Oh, no, don't tell me that you've conscripted Elliot into this manhunt?"

"As a matter of fact, why don't you come over to dinner Friday night and just see? Consider it first-hand research. Maybe you won't end up using Elliot after all."

"Harrumph! If I used any man I'd ever met as a model for one of my heroes—other than Elliot, of course—my readers would have fits. They don't want beer-drinking, potbellied heroes, George. For heaven's sake, they live with reality! They want the closest thing to a perfect man I can come up with.''

"I know. Masterful, gentle, tender, a great lover, arrogant, of course, to add flavor—"

"You got it. There ain't nothin' like that around nowadays, I promise you. Even Elliot snores, I'll bet, and gets nasty every now and again.''

"Sometimes, and not yet. Chelsea, surely you—" George broke off abruptly at the pain in her lower back. "Drat. Not again. I swear this kiddo is going to do me in.''

Chelsea bounded up from the sofa, all concern. "You want me to rub your back?''

"No, I'll be fine in a minute. That's one of Elliot's favorite chores, Ben-Gaying my back. Now will you be here for dinner on Friday?''

"Oh, all right. I can't imagine what you're going to drag in here.''

"Trust me," George said.

On Friday morning Elliot Mallory, chairman of radiology, made his way down to the emergency room, only to be told that Dr. David Winter was over at Mulberry Union, swimming.

It was a bit early for Elliot's daily laps, but he knew his duty and swiftly changed into his swim trunks and dove into the pool. He didn't stop David until after he'd completed ten laps.

"Elliot! I thought you were an afternooner.''

"I am usually," Elliot said. "You got a minute, David?''

"Sure.''

Both men swam to the side of the pool and hoisted themselves onto the tiled apron.

"What's up? You got a special case? A problem only I can handle?"

"Nope, and don't sound so hopeful." Damn, but this was embarrassing as hell. He still couldn't quite figure out how George had wrung the promise from him. Well, there was no hope for it. "You busy tonight, David?"

David grinned wryly. "I was going for drinks with a couple of colleagues. Bores, both of them. You have something better to offer?"

"As a matter of fact, I just might. You want to come over to dinner?"

David looked distinctly wary. "Do you mind me asking who's doing the cooking?"

Elliot laughed, remembering David's only venture into George's cooking. "Come on, so the chicken was a little dry and the peas a bit hard."

"Thank God you made the Irish coffee and the cheesecake."

"I guess I agree with you. Let me reassure you that tonight I'm going to be the chef. I promise you a feast to add two pounds."

"I don't mean to sound ungrateful, Elliot. Lord knows George is the most—hey, wait a minute." He studied Elliot's face for a long moment. "All right, who else is coming to dinner?"

"A friend of George's. A very nice woman. A very attractive woman."

David groaned. "All right, I'll bite. What's this attractive, very nice woman's name?"

"Chelsea Lattimer. She's around twenty-eight, never been married, tousled, curly black hair, blue eyes—maybe they're green—but in any case, she's okay, David, I swear." He didn't add that Chelsea

Lattimer was occasionally quite outrageous and out-spoken. He'd teased her once that he was going to send her to London so she could take the speaker's corner in Hyde Park.

"Well, it's not as if I'm out on the town every night. Lord, this has been a long year!"

And lonely as hell, I'll just bet, Elliot thought silently. David Winter had been seduced by the University Medical Center to come from Boston to become chief of the trauma section. They hadn't become particularly close friends until after Elliot's marriage to George only two months before. The previous six months had seen Elliot sunk in oceans of self-pity, when he wasn't being a snarling dictator to his staff and an arrogant ass to his colleagues.

"Seven o'clock?" Elliot asked.

"You got it. Want to do some more laps?"

"Let's go." He grinned as he slid into the water. "At least you're more of a challenge than George ever was."

Chelsea looked at her image in the mirror. You look like a crow, she told herself. Stop it, Chels! If you compare yourself to your heroines or to gorgeous George, you'll crawl in the closet and never come out.

Well, maybe I'm not too bad. She ran her brush through her thick hair once more, only to see the irrepressible black curls bounce up in different directions. Tangled glory, that's what I've got. Now how about that for an absurd title? Sure beats *Passion's Pulsing Pleasures*, or *Torpid Tender Trials*.

She laughed, gave herself a thumbs-up sign in the mirror and was out of her Sausalito condo in five minutes. It was only a twenty minute ride over the

Golden Gate into the city. George and Elliot had moved to his old restored Victorian upon their marriage—only because his was larger, George had assured her. And, of course, George had added, it was so much less plastic and modern than her condo.

As Chelsea wove her way onto Lombard Street she remembered George's words. *Trust me.* Well, since Elliot was such a beautiful man, George certainly wouldn't stick her with a gnome. Would she? Maybe George had lost her objectivity, being eight months' pregnant and all.

She turned right onto Divisidero and headed up into Pacific Heights. This is where I'd live, she thought, if I ever moved out of Sausalito. The view from the top of the hill was breathtaking—all beautiful Bay, Alcatraz, Angel Island and, of course, her beloved Sausalito. She pulled into the Mallorys' driveway ten minutes early. She recognized George's Porsche, Esmerelda, and Elliot's Jaguar, whose unlikely appellation was Cock and Bull. No other cars. So the newest Don Juan doctor of San Francisco hadn't arrived yet. Just as well.

The splendid Mallorys, as she had termed them in her mind, met her with great enthusiasm and plunked her down on the sofa with a white wine, all within five minutes.

"Elliot's making his famous fresh garden bisque soup, Caesar salad, apricot basted ham—"

"Peach, George."

"Yes, peach basted ham—"

"That's all I need," Chelsea interrupted, waving her hand. "Can't you cut out the croutons from the salad, Elliot?"

"Croutons?" George asked. "What's that?"

Elliot laughed, tweaked his wife's perfect nose and said, "That's those little fried pieces of day-old French bread, love. Sorry, Chelsea, but you gotta eat it the way I serve it. What are you worried about? You're a skinny little twit."

"With computer derriere," Chelsea said.

"Oh, bother," George said. "Here I am looking like the proverbial spider and you're worried about having a rounded butt!"

"Exactly," Elliot said.

"If I could manage to heave myself out of this chair, you jerk, I'd make you eat your words!"

"You'd make me eat *exactly*?" Elliot asked, looking innocently bewildered.

"I think I will have a wine spritzer now, servant," George said.

"Don't get huffy, wife, or I won't Ben-Gay you tonight."

Elliot turned in the doorway. "A spider, huh? Maybe that's why I like to rub your back. My vision is limited."

George fell back in her chair, groaning. "Are you sure you want to get married, Chels? Just look at what I have to put up with."

But Chelsea was gazing wistfully after Elliot. "You're so lucky, George," she said with a sigh.

"Yes, I know, but it took the dratted man long enough to realize it. Ah, there's the doorbell, Chelsea. Would you get it? By the time I get myself out of this chair the poor man will think he's got the wrong house and leave."

"You're not George," the man said when Chelsea opened the front door.

"No," she said. "Neither are you." And thank God you're not a gnome.

He looked a bit taken aback, then smiled. "No, I'm David Winter. And you, I take it, are Chelsea Lattimer."

Chelsea nodded and stepped aside. Goodness, she thought, he's not bad-looking. No, not at all. She felt like a shrimp standing beside him, armpit height, she thought. He looked like a reasonable facsimile of a hero. His hair was a lovely chestnut color and his eyes a real hazel, nothing wishy-washy and in between.

"Good grief, George," she heard his deep voice boom from the living room, "I'm not a gynecologist! Please, don't do anything we'll regret this evening."

"Such a sweet-talking man," George said. "Hello, David. You've met Chelsea?"

"Yeah," Chelsea said. "He determined that I'm not you."

"Dear me, if you were, you'd be in deep trouble!"

George beamed at the two of them. A very nice couple, she thought, though David did look very proper in his three-piece suit, complete with white shirt and tie. And Chelsea, marvelous, of course, but very Marin casual in her dark blue corduroy jeans and white knit sweater. She cleared her throat. "I think I'll help Elliot in the kitchen."

To Chelsea's surprise David laughed deeply. "Please, George, don't! Just stay where you are. Trust Elliot, please."

Elliot emerged from the kitchen and greeted David. "A white wine?"

"Fine with me."

"I'll be with you guys in just a minute." He called over his shoulder, "Don't worry, Chelsea. I bought two bottles of Chablis just for you."

"Well," David said after a moment. "It's a pleasure to meet a friend of the Mallorys'. Do you live here in the city?"

"No, in Sausalito."

David's eyes brightened with interest. "It's a beautiful town. I've been looking around there for a house. What part?"

"On Bridgeway. In a condominium complex called Whiskey Springs."

"I've got my sailboat docked just across from you," David said. "We're practically neighbors. But I'm not interested in a condo."

"No, of course not," Chelsea agreed. Perfectly innocuous conversation, idiot. But he made a condo sound like something from the slums. Your turn. Men love to talk about themselves. "You're a doctor?"

"Yes. I've been out here less than a year, actually. I hail from Boston."

"I went to school in Boston," Chelsea said.

"There are so many. Which one?"

"The best one," Chelsea said, tilting her chin up just a bit. "Boston College."

"Oh. An excellent school."

"Did you go to school in Boston?"

"Just medical school. Harvard."

"Oh." A stuffed-shirt former preppie. She should have guessed. "And you were on staff at Mass General?"

"Why, yes. How did you know?"

It fits. "Just a guess. You did undergraduate at Princeton? Yale?"

"Princeton."

"Where did you go to prep school?"

"Andover."

Lord, did it all fit! Well, keep him talking. He was a joy to look at. "Why did you come West?"

"A great offer."

"It must have been a big change."

"Yes, a very big one," he said. He continued to George, "When's the baby due?"

"In four weeks exactly, thank God."

"Is Elliot driving you nuts?"

"No," George said in some disgust, "at least, not in the way you mean. I think he wonders why I'm not still jogging."

Elliot, who had just come into the living room bearing a tray with drinks on it, grinned and said, "I was thinking that I could build her something like a skateboard and she could make her way around on her stomach. She'd certainly be high enough off the sidewalk."

"That boggles the imagination, Elliot." Chelsea laughed.

David became quiet, his thoughts on the very happy couple. And Elliot won't be just a father, he was thinking, he'll be a parent. David had just realized in the past ten months how much he didn't know about his own two children. Sure, he thought, I'm a great father. Haven't I provided them with everything? He shook away his depressing thoughts and looked at Chelsea Lattimer. He felt as if she'd given him the third degree and he'd flunked. Well, he had a long evening ahead of him, and after all, didn't women like to talk about themselves?

"Well," George said brightly, taking away his chance to speak, "how's the beans, doc?"

"Actually, French green beans, George, with pearl onions and slivered almonds," Elliot said.

"Here I was hoping for hot dogs and chips."

There was a brief pause, and Chelsea blurted out, "What kind of a doctor are you?"

"Now I'm chief of the trauma section at the university. I hang out mostly in the emergency room when I'm not in the OR."

"It means," Elliot said, "that he's a damned fine surgeon and has an uncanny and much needed flair for organization."

"Oh," Chelsea said. She'd heard that surgeons, or blades, were normally an obnoxious breed, full of themselves and their great talent. Oh, well, it was just for one evening. Let him keep talking; it would make the time go more quickly. He sent her a smile at that moment that looked anything but obnoxious, and Chelsea found herself smiling back.

"Are you from California, Miss Lattimer?" David asked.

"Chelsea, and yes, from Santa Barbara. My folks still live there."

Aha, David thought. A native Californian and probably so laid back she'd sneer at anything or anyone from the pseudointellectual East Coast.

"Chelsea's dad is a dentist," George said.

"You've got brothers and sisters?"

"Nope, I'm their one and only. I think they gave me one look and decided not to press their luck."

"I'm an only child, too," David said. "My parents couldn't have more children, though I understand they wanted to."

It still fits, Chelsea thought. Produce a son whose first words were probably "conservative" and "rich," and of course they'd want to produce a veritable battalion.

"Naturally," Chelsea said aloud.

That earned her a raised, questioning eyebrow from David Winter. Elliot called them to order then, and they trooped to the table.

"I still can't figure out," George said after everyone was served, "how Elliot can time everything so it's all hot when it hits the table."

"Natural male superiority," Elliot said. "Don't you agree, David?"

"With the dirty look I just got from Chelsea, I think I'll keep my opinions to myself."

"I thought," Chelsea said, annoyed, "that surgeons especially, always gave their opinions, asked for or not."

"Surgeons are just men," David said.

"And women," Chelsea added quickly.

Elliot shot David a rueful look. "We're surrounded by career women, David. Guess we'd better watch our step."

"There are more and more women doctors," David said stiffly. "Most of them, however, still don't go into surgery."

"And why do you think that's the case?" Chelsea asked.

Never in his life had he been asked such a question by another person, much less by a woman he'd just met. Just who the hell did she think she was, anyway? A flaky California rich girl, probably. Sausalito wasn't a cheap place to live, after all. Still, it wouldn't be polite to put her soundly in her place. And his Boston

Brahmin parents had taught him manners. He said easily, "Perhaps women don't like such a demanding schedule."

"Or perhaps," Chelsea said, "they aren't given the opportunity. I read an article last year that gave the appalling rate of suicide among women residents in surgery."

"It's a very difficult pace to maintain," David said, proud of himself for his display of patience. "And training takes a long time. I venture to say that most women would prefer doing other things than training for five years or so."

"You mean like having babies?"

"That, yes."

"Would you like some more Caesar salad, David?" George asked, shooting a look at her friend. Chelsea should realize that there would be time enough to infuriate him after she got to know him better.

He shook his head, even as Chelsea said, "Don't you see a place for a bit of compromise, doctor?"

"In medicine? There's been quite a bit already." His tone implied to Chelsea that there'd been far too much.

"But if women didn't compromise enough, men wouldn't be born and have the chance not to compromise."

Elliot laughed and rolled his eyes at his wife. "Your point is well taken, Chelsea, if I understand it."

"I'm certain that an intelligent, open-minded male of the species could," she said.

"Perhaps," David said, wanting to smooth things over, "women have different priorities. A family, children..."

"Men don't count family and children as a priority?"

"That isn't what I meant!" Damned pushy female! He thought with some fondness of drinking with the two boring colleagues. Both male. Neither with a big mouth.

Chelsea, receiving an agonized look from George, forced herself to retrench. But she didn't want to. She wanted to smack the righteous look off his handsome face. "Delicious dinner, Elliot," she said, sending him a dazzling smile.

Outrageous female! David thought. Probably never worked a day in her pampered life. What the hell did she know about priorities, responsibility and achievement?

Chelsea polished off another glass of white wine. She was inevitably feeling more mellow, and a bit guilty. David Winter still appeared as good-looking as he had when she first laid eyes on him, but he was a stuffed shirt, damn it. But, her thinking continued, she had antagonized him, challenged him, made things a bit uncomfortable. I'll back off a bit, she decided.

After the delicious meal George excused both herself and Chelsea and hauled her friend upstairs. George whirled on her friend the moment she'd closed the bedroom door. "You're being obnoxious, Chelsea, and you know it. You probably took a dislike to David on your drive over here, didn't you?"

"He's a stuffed shirt and a preppie," Chelsea said defensively.

"A bit, maybe, but you've been attacking him as if he were Hitler himself! For goodness' sake, give the poor fellow a chance!"

"You think I should change my stripes, huh?"

"You have so many to choose from!"

"You're right, George," Chelsea said, appearing much struck. She added thoughtfully, smiling impishly, "I think I'll try my fluffy, feminine, helpless stripes for the rest of the evening. Maybe it'll loosen up our three-piece-suited preppie doctor from Boston. It's probably exactly what he's used to from women."

"Don't go overboard," George warned as they made their way back downstairs. "He's not stupid."

They heard the men laughing in the living room. David, having added Irish coffee to his three glasses of wine, was feeling no pain. He was stretched out on the floor in front of the fireplace, laughing at one of Elliot's stories.

It took him a good ten minutes to realize that Chelsea Lattimer had ceased her obnoxious comments. Had she indeed been obnoxious? He wasn't so sure now. Indeed, she was laughing enthusiastically at every story and joke he told.

Over more Irish coffee Chelsea, at George's encouragement, waxed eloquent on her ill-fated experience with an interior decorator whose dearest love was to place Dresden shepherdesses on every available surface. Women, David thought, but without rancor this time. All they're interested in is spending money. But she was cute, a bit giddy after all that wine, but that just seemed to add to her burgeoning charm. He watched her dark blue eyes sparkle at a bout of repartee between George and Elliot and decided that this bit of female fluff would be quite nice in bed. Lord knew it had been a long time.

Elliot pulled out Trivial Pursuit and matched himself up with Chelsea. Chelsea, quite aware that Dr.

David Winter was nearly as mellow as she, decided to continue her role as the cute lamebrain. She felt sorry for Elliot. They were trounced throughly. But no one really cared. Too much wine had passed down all their respective throats, except George, who had had only a wine spritzer.

"Lord, look at the time," Chelsea said, blinking owlishly down at her watch. "It's nearly one in the morning!"

As they'd all been lounging on the floor during the game, David had gotten quite a good look at Chelsea's legs. Very nice. Very nice, indeed.

"Yes, it is late," he agreed. "I think I'd like to follow you home, Chelsea, if that's okay with you."

He'd taken off his tie and coat, and Chelsea was looking fondly at his muscled forearms. "All right," she said. If he wanted to play masterful protector, it was just fine with her. Maybe he wasn't such a stuffed shirt after all.

They reached her condo some thirty minutes later. Chelsea was sober as a judge. George accused her of having a hollow leg, and she supposed it was true when it came to white wine. She wondered, looking at David as he came toward her from his car, if the same could be said about him. His very nice hazel eyes were a bit glazed.

He stopped about three inches from her and gave her what could only be called a scorching look. "Come here," he said, and drew her into his arms.

Merciful heavens, she thought, one of my heroes couldn't do it any better.

Chapter 2

His mouth was hard and aggressive, and his hands were quickly stroking down her back to curve around her hips.

Her heroes wouldn't do that! Oh, yes, they would, she amended to herself. Most of them were arrogant, conceited, masterful, out and out rakes, she supposed.

Well, this wasn't the eighteenth century!

His mouth suddenly gentled, and for an instant, but just an instant, she responded.

"You're such a sweet little thing," he said against her lips, and pulled her closer.

"Sweet little what?" Dear heavens, was that sterling bit of endearment his introduction to bed?

David raised his head, feeling a bit dazed. She squirmed away from him, and he reluctantly dropped his hands from her very nice bottom.

"I don't know," he said truthfully. "I guess I got a bit carried away."

"Do all preppie doctors from Boston act like they're God's gift to women?"

David's wits returned with some rapidity. He stared down at her. She was sounding like the woman he'd first met. He felt frustrated and a bit angry. "I don't think I'm mistaken, Miss Lattimer. You rather liked what I was doing until—" He broke off in amazement. "You're a tease," he said. "A damned tease. You led me on...."

"I'm not a tease! You're a conceited idiot. If you will remember, Dr. Winter, I didn't know you existed before five hours ago! Well, maybe it was six hours. And just because I was nice to you and listened to your stupid jokes, you believe I want to hop in the sack!"

"What I think is that you're weird," David gritted between clenched teeth. "I would think by the time a woman reached your age, she was through with game playing."

Had Chelsea been sitting in front of her computer, her fingers would have been drumming a wild tattoo on the keys. "You might look like a hero," she said, "but your character leaves a great deal to be desired. Now why don't you go to your precious hospital and fondle a patient!"

"Fondle a patient! Of all the ridiculous—"

"Good night, Dr. Winter." She slammed her key into the lock and was thankful when it turned on the first try. "Don't forget to fasten your seat belt!"

David stared a moment at the slammed door. Damn you, Elliot, he thought. How could you set me up with a nut case? And a probable schizophrenic. From obnoxious to fluff-head to tease.

* * *

"He's a no-conversation lecher!"

George looked thoughtfully at Chelsea, who was pacing ferociously about the Mallorys' living room the following Tuesday afternoon.

"I think David is rather amusing," George said. "Lord knows he's very nice to look at."

"What do you know about it?" Chelsea said in a nasty voice. "The only person you hear or see is your damned husband. How could you set me up with that—"

"That what, Chels? Talk about changing your stripes! You made the man feel like he was the most marvelous male specimen in the universe. What did you expect him to do? Kiss your hand at the front door and sweep you a courtly bow?"

Chelsea groused under her breath, finally admitting, "Well, maybe I did go just a bit overboard with the fluffy, air-head feminine act, but—"

"But what? I think you're being unfair. David may be just a bit reserved, but according to Elliot, he's an excellent doctor, has a good sense of humor and deals well with the emergency room staff, which I imagine, can't be a barrel of roses."

"Apples," Chelsea said. "Bed of roses. He called me a tease, the jerk!"

"He's a good kisser, huh?"

"I didn't hang around long enough to really check him out. Well, maybe just a little bit, to punish him for being such a nerd." That really hadn't been the case at all, but Chelsea wasn't about to change now. She was on a roll.

George burst into laughter. "Oh, Chels, I wish you could hear yourself! It's too much! Please, get yourself a glass of white wine. I can't bear all this useless energy."

Two glasses of white wine later, Chelsea was sitting cross-legged on the living room floor, looking thoughtfully at George. "You really think he deserves another chance?"

"I most certainly do," George said. "Why don't we try again, say this Friday night? And, Chels, why don't you wear your own stripes. You know, the natural, fun, loving ones, and no changing in the middle of the river."

"Stream," Chelsea said. "And it's horses, not stripes." She added, her voice glum, "Dr. Winter probably doesn't care for natural, fun, or loving."

"Just give it a shot."

"Look, David, it was all a mistake. George told me Chelsea had the flu. That's probably why you found her behavior a little weird. She was taking antihistamines and drinking, which isn't too bright, admittedly. That would make anyone odd. You did think she was okay, didn't you?"

"Look, Elliot, she's a conceited little rich girl, just like—well, just like some women I've known. She's probably never done an ounce of work in her life, and she's got the nicest bot—" He broke off as a resident approached. After a quick discussion the resident left.

"I've got to go, Elliot. A traffic accident."

"About Friday night?"

"All right. Seven o'clock."

Chelsea, lost in San Francisco in the year 1854, didn't hear the telephone until the fifth ring. Sarah Butler, her part-time housekeeper, companion, phone answerer and good friend, was across the street at the grocery store, buying radishes for some unlikely concoction that would have only ninety-five calories in it.

It was George. "Hi, Chels. Hope I didn't interrupt you, but everything is go for Friday."

"I can't believe David Winter ever wants to see me again."

"Well, he does, and he'll be here with bells on."

"More likely another three-piece charcoal gray suit with a pearl-colored silk tie and a starchy white shirt."

"My, what a memory you have for a man you didn't particularly like."

"All writers have excellent memories," Chelsea said with great, but instant, untruth.

"Sure, and all cats eat Alpo."

"Now that's bizarre, George."

"I know. Get back to the novel. I'll see you soon."

"Chelsea," David said stiffly as he trailed behind Elliot into the Mallorys' living room.

"Hello, David," Chelsea said, looking up from the sofa with a show of mild interest. Oddly enough, she felt a bit nervous, a very unusual state for her, and her voice sounded clipped as she said, "How have you been this past week?"

"Busy. Very busy."

"How interesting."

Yeah, you sound fascinated, David thought, but said nothing. "You feeling okay, George?" he asked, turning to his hostess.

George's back was throbbing more than usual, but she gave David her flawless smile. "Just fine, David."

"Are you over your flu, Chelsea?" he asked.

Chelsea looked at him blankly. George said in a very carrying voice, "Elliot! Where are you? We've got starving folk in here!"

"Ah," Elliot said, emerging with a tray of goodies from the kitchen, "a man's work is never done. At least I'm not barefoot or looking like a spider."

"Jerk," George said with high good humor. "Why," she asked, examining the tray, "is this cheese spread on crackers?"

"Wash out your mouth, woman!" Elliot added to David, "She does know the difference, I think. It's my special homemade cheese ragomontade, artfully set on gourmet wheat—"

George giggled. "Stop that, you're making it up. There's no such thing as ragomontade!"

"Delicious," Chelsea said, "whatever it is. Do you cook, Dr. Winter?"

He arched a brow at her. "Sorry, it's a skill I never acquired."

"Ah, you found a wife to drudge for you, huh?" As soon as the words were out of her mouth she cursed herself silently. Why did she react to him with instant sarcasm?

"Elliot," George sang out, "could you pour Chelsea some white wine?"

"Yes, I did find a wife," David said, "but she didn't cook, either." Take that, you lovely-bottomed, smart-mouthed woman! My God, he thought, looking at her closely, she was blushing!

Despite the reddened cheeks, David had to admit that Chelsea Lattimer looked quite lovely. He was sure he'd think so even if he weren't so horny. She was wearing a yellow silk dress with black doodles on it, and high-heeled black shoes. She'd probably come up

to his Adam's apple, he thought. It occurred to him
that she must want to make amends. She was certainly dressed to impress.

He discounted his own impeccable appearance.

Elliot shot his wife an "I'm going to get you for
this" look, but George just smiled sweetly at him.
How could he have fallen for that flu bit? "Chelsea
was just telling us her latest plot when you arrived,
David."

That drew a startled look. "Plot?" he asked, giving her his full attention. "I don't understand. You're
a writer?"

"Yes."

"You're published?"

He didn't have to sound so bloody incredulous,
Chelsea thought. "Why, yes." She added modestly, "I
was very lucky. In the right place at the right time with
the right manuscript, and all that."

"Oh, bosh, Chels," George said. "She never got
even one rejection slip, David. The very first publishing house she went to signed her up immediately."

"Which hardcover house are you with?" David
asked.

"I'm not. I'm original paperback."

"Oh. Mass market. Well, there are plenty of fine
novels in paperback."

"Of course, and the distribution is so much greater.
One would rather have two hundred thousand readers instead of just five thousand."

Two hundred thousand! Was that just a number
she'd used for illustration? David blinked. Had she
bought that condo in Sausalito with her own money,
then, and not Daddy's? Why the hell hadn't Elliot told

him she was a writer? He shot Elliot a look, which was blandly ignored.

"Perhaps I've read your work," he said. "What name do you use?"

"My own. Chelsea Lattimer."

"Sorry, but I'll keep an eye out. What do you write? Fiction? Nonfiction? Biographies?"

Chelsea looked him straight in the eye. "Fiction. I write long historical novels. The ones filled with adventure, intrigue, lots of romance—"

"And delicious sex," George added, rolling her eyes.

David blurted out before he could stop himself, his voice filled with incredulous distaste, "You write *romance* novels?"

"Yes, I do," Chelsea said. "May I have some more wine, George?" Time out, she thought. Oh, Lord, what should she do now?

"Certainly, Chels."

Chelsea forced herself to drink slowly from her newly filled glass.

David fidgeted with his whiskey for a moment. "Do you plan to switch to more . . . literary work in the future?"

"Exactly what do you mean, David?" Chelsea asked, not moving a muscle.

"Well, really, Chelsea, that stuff is drivel. It's pap for idiots and frustrated women—"

"I'm not a frustrated idiot, David," George said, winking at Chelsea.

"What do you read, David?" Chelsea asked. "Or perhaps I should say, do you read?"

Elliot seated himself on the arm of his wife's chair. He was grinning; he couldn't help it. He felt rather sorry for David, who was quickly digging a hole so deep he'd have to use a bullhorn to call someone to come to rescue him.

"Well, of course I read. Good literature, the classics, biographies and some bestsellers."

"Which bestsellers?"

"Well, you know, this and that. Whatever is on the *New York Times* Best Seller list, I suppose."

"Ah, you're led by what other people think," Chelsea said. "Don't you have any favorite authors? People you've picked yourself?"

He knew he was fitting himself for his own coffin, but her damned calm, patronizing attitude was too much. "Yes, I like to read Westerns, as a matter of fact. Westerns, of course, aren't exactly great literature, but they have value, good plots, historical insights—"

"My novels also have good plots, historical insights and accuracy."

"But it's tripe! Good grief, men and women never behaved the way those novels have them behave!"

"Have you ever read one?"

"Certainly not," he snapped.

"Why not? As a doctor, it would seem to me to be the epitome of idiocy to draw a conclusion based on not one shred of evidence, or, if you will, make a diagnosis without examining the patient."

"It's not the same thing," he said. He shot Elliot a look of sheer desperation, but Elliot only smiled at him blandly.

"I don't particularly care for Westerns, but at least I've given them a try," Chelsea went on. "At least half a dozen, I'd say. Why isn't it the same thing?"

"Men are better...no—" David plowed his fingers through his hair. "It's just that men's literature is more accurate, more entertaining—"

"Are you saying that women's literature has less entertainment value, less accuracy, than men's literature?"

"It's not true to life."

"You lived in the 1860s? Or shot up a town marshal?"

"Of course not," David said. "Look, Chelsea, can we drop this? I'm sorry if I've insulted the type of novel you write. All right?"

"Certainly," Chelsea said, giving him an "I just tromped you into the ground smile." She wanted to laugh when he practically ground his teeth. "I'll just bet you hated *Romeo and Juliet* and only go to the movies to see people get shot full of holes."

David, unwisely, didn't ignore that aside. "I loved the play and see all kinds of movies," he said, his voice very cool.

"Well, people need romance, all people. Even you, Dr. Winter, must have had those marvelous, romantic feelings with a woman you loved or were infatuated with. Unfortunately, for many people those intense feelings don't last. That's why they read books and go to movies. It fills a need, it presents an ideal, brings back their own memories. Life is sometimes too bereft of—"

"Bull," David said.

"I hope both of you have sharpened your appetites," Elliot said, rising. "Dinner's ready, if I don't mistake my nose. Come on, George, let me heave you out of that chair and into the dining room."

Over spaghetti that tasted like heaven come to earth, David asked George when she would be returning to modeling and TV.

"In November. I'll only be traveling one week a month, so my husband here can't get into too much trouble in my absence."

"You find modeling acceptable?" Chelsea couldn't resist asking David as she crunched into a delicious slice of garlic bread.

"For a woman," he said, grinning at her. "I meant to tell you," he continued to Chelsea, "you look gorgeous tonight. Silk becomes you."

"It's sixty percent polyester," Chelsea said.

"I like a woman who's cheap to keep."

Chelsea laughed. Perhaps he wasn't such a bigoted, intolerant stuffed shirt after all. Perhaps he had a modicum of wit.

Elliot asked George a question, and when she didn't answer, all eyes at the table turned toward her.

"Elliot," George said with great calm, "I think the kiddo is going to come soon."

Elliot turned perfectly white. "But it's three weeks too soon! How do you know, George?" He was out of his chair as he spoke.

"Contractions," George said. "At least we got through dinner," she added, giving her husband a tense smile.

"You love spaghetti," Elliot said wildly. "I was wondering why you were eating like a bird. Oh, God!"

"Who's your doctor, George?" David asked calmly.

"Maggie Smith, at the university."

"What's her number?"

George looked at him helplessly. "It's evening. I don't know. Oh, wait, it's in my address book. I forgot that Maggie insisted—"

"Where's the address book, George?"

She told him. David turned to Elliot. "Why don't you bundle George up and take her to the hospital? I'll call Dr. Smith and meet you there."

Twenty minutes later David pulled his Lancia into the parking garage at the hospital.

"The baby is three weeks early," Chelsea said.

"Probably just as well," David said as he helped her from the car. "She was getting awfully big, and her pelvis doesn't look all that accommodating."

"You never lost your cool. I couldn't think of a thing to say or do. I'm a disaster in an emergency."

"I have two children of my own, a great deal of training and George isn't my wife," David said.

Chelsea shot him a look, but said nothing. He had said that he'd been married. Two children? Were they in Boston with their mother? What had happened to their marriage? Whatever, thank God for his cool, matter-of-fact conduct.

When they reached the waiting room on the fifth floor, a nurse told them that Dr. Smith was with Elliot and George, and that Mrs. Mallory was doing nicely.

"Want a cup of coffee?" David asked.

"How can you be so calm about all this? Oh, yes, your training. I'm sorry. Yes, thank you."

"It's a natural process, Chelsea," he said patiently. "George is young and very healthy, and she doesn't drink white wine," he added.

He left her to get coffee.

"And I don't drink whiskey," she muttered to his retreating back.

Elliot came into the waiting room ten minutes later, looking less distracted. "All's well," he said. "Look, you guys don't have to hang around. Maggie thinks it's going to take a while."

"Both my children were born at the crack of dawn," David said.

"Does George hurt?" Chelsea asked, ignoring David's words.

"She's handling everything just fine. We did Lamaze."

"I think I'll stay around," Chelsea said.

"Me, too," David added.

"It's up to you," Elliot said, running his fingers through his thick dark hair. "I'll come out with progress reports when I can."

"I think," David said slowly, "that the birth process is just as hard on men as it is on women."

Chelsea could only stare at him. "You're kidding," she said finally.

"What I meant was that the waiting is wretched."

"That's true," Chelsea conceded. "If it were my choice, though, I'd rather do the waiting than the yelling."

David winced a bit at that.

"Did you do Lamaze with your wife?"

"No," he said, his voice suddenly terse and chilly. "Margaret didn't want to." He added, a touch of bitterness in his voice, "I didn't get to see my children born."

"I'm sorry," Chelsea said for want of anything better. Deep waters, she thought, and murky. "How old are your kids?"

"Mark is eight, and Taylor is six."

"Two boys, huh?"

"No, Taylor's my daughter. Taylor is an old family name."

"You must miss them very much."

"Yes, yes, I do," David said. He hadn't seen them in six months, since he'd gone back to Boston to visit. And he hadn't stayed all that long. Margaret drove him bananas. He tried a smile. "I wish we had a deck of cards."

"What's your game?" Chelsea asked, a definite fleecing light in her blue eyes.

His smile widened. "Poker. Five-card stud."

"If you like," Chelsea said in an offhand manner, "you can come to our monthly poker game. This month—next week, in fact—it's at my house in Sausalito."

"Just who attends this poker game?"

"Don't sound so wary! I'll just bet you're picturing a bunch of giggling females, gossiping while they toss cards around."

"Something like that."

"How old are you, David?" she asked him abruptly.

"Thirty-six," he said. "Why?"

"I was just wondering how long it takes a man to develop so many ridiculous assumptions."

"I was always a quick study," he said, grinning at her.

Chapter 3

George was reading about the Romanovs," Elliot said to David the next day in the hospital cafeteria. "Our son's name is Alexander Nicholas, which is close enough for jazz, I suppose. I guess it beats Lance or Stud."

David raised his cup of coffee. "Congratulations, and the name is quite a handle. George is feeling okay today?"

"She's got the energy of a tiger, which is frightening as hell. She was already out of bed this morning, staring in the nursery window."

"Is she breast-feeding?"

Elliot shook his head. "Her career prohibits it. Can't have a cover girl all filled with milk, you know."

"My wife breast-fed our kids," David said. "Her mother deemed it appropriate."

Elliot looked at David intently and felt a pang of concern. He sounded depressed as hell. "Your kids coming out for the Christmas holiday?"

"Yep. I can't imagine how they're going to adjust to laid back California."

"They'll have a blast, you'll see. Speaking of laid back, did you get Chelsea home all right last night? Rather, at dawn?"

"No, she had her own car. I assume she got home all right." David fiddled with his Styrofoam cup, shredding the rim. After all the interminable waiting during the previous night, they'd come to a truce, of sorts. She'd been almost mellow, and stone sober. He added, "She invited me over this Friday for her monthly poker game."

If Elliot hadn't been so tired and preoccupied, he would have said something to that, probably issued a red alert, but he didn't. He said only, "You'll have an interesting time, I'm sure."

"You look like hell, Elliot. Go home and get some sleep."

The PA system came alive suddenly. "Dr. Winter to ER, stat."

David rose immediately. "Give my love to George, and my blessing to the perfect baby."

Elsa Perkins was efficient, cute and coming on to him. She was a very young nurse, just out of training, but she had the fortitude and stomach of a seasoned trooper, which were necessary to serve in an emergency room. Their patient was a boy with second-degree burns, who, with his friends, had wanted to try some black magic in the family garage. The kids had hung black towels over the windows, lit candles around a crate cum altar—and promptly set the place on fire. The parents were having a fit in the waiting room.

"Okay, champ," David said, gently patting the boy's shoulder. "You're gonna be just fine, but you're not going to feel like slaying any dragons for a while, or burning any more candles. You just lie still while I talk to your folks. Do you hurt anymore?"

The boy had wide brown eyes that were beginning to glaze over from the painkiller. He shook his head.

"Good job, Elsa," David said. "Stay with him until he's out, all right?"

"Certainly, doctor," she replied.

He spoke soothingly to the parents, then talked briefly with the doctor from the burn unit upstairs. The boy was stable, thank the Lord, and with a couple of skin grafts on his legs, he'd be just fine.

Ten minutes later David went into the operating room for three hours, suturing up the belly of a man who'd had his riding lawn mower roll over on him.

Then there was a woman carried in by her white-faced husband, bleeding profusely from what turned out to be a miscarriage. David, an intern and a nurse were covered with her blood before they got her stabilized.

It was nearly ten o'clock in the evening when he finally stopped, drew a deep breath and realized that he was starving.

"I brought you a corned beef sandwich, doctor," said Elsa, giving him her special smile.

"You read my mind," he said, grinning. "Thank you."

"You work so hard." He recognized her tone as "just out of nursing school" doctor worship.

"So do you," he said in a crisp voice. "Sandwich is great. Thanks again."

Her look said clearly that she'd get him anything he wanted, and he carefully gave all his attention to his sandwich. When he was finished, she smiled again.

"Well," he said, standing up and stretching. "At least we didn't lose anyone today."

Elsa's smile fell away. "I'm sorry, Dr. Winter. The older woman who came in earlier with chest pains... she died."

"Damn," David said.

By the time Friday night arrived David didn't care whether or not Chelsea Lattimer's poker party was a group of gossiping women or a troupe of singing parrots. He realized as he drove over the Golden Gate Bridge toward Sausalito that he'd missed her, crazy woman that she doubtless was. He'd called her once, but had gotten her answering machine. He hated answering machines and hadn't left a message.

Chelsea showered, dressed and exchanged her small diamond stud earrings for some gold loops, all within fifteen minutes. The earrings took the longest. She'd just had the nerve to get her ears pierced three months before, and she was still chicken about changing earrings. She stared a moment at the small gold loops. Gives me a certain pizzazz, she decided, and shook her head to make them jingle a bit, which they didn't.

Another fifteen minutes and she was walking out of her small kitchen carrying two trays of goodies—guacamole, tortilla chips and onion dip. The onion dip was for Maurice, her gay interior decorator friend from the city who wouldn't touch anything that was *green*. Sarah, her housekeeper, made it especially for

him each time he came over. His real name was Elvin,
he'd told her once when he was more than eight sheets
to the wind.

He's late, Chelsea thought forty-five minutes later.
He probably won't be coming. She, Maurice, Delbert—an over-the-hill jockey who used to race at Golden Gate Fields—and Angelo—an exporter of Chinese
oddities who had a shop on Union Street—had already settled down for serious play.

When the doorbell rang she jumped and dropped
her cards. Maurice yelped. "Good God, Chels! A full
house! Lord, guys, talk about being saved by the
bell!"

"Stick it, Maurice. It's David Winter. Please, please
be reasonable and not too crazy, all right?"

Why am I so nervous? she wondered, unconsciously pulling down her pink wool sweater. "Hi"
was all she could think of to say when she opened her
front door. Lord, he looked gorgeous. He was wearing casual corduroy jeans and a ribbed navy sweater.

"Sorry I'm late," David said, shoving a paper bag
toward her, "but I stopped to buy some cookies and
a bottle of white wine."

She smiled up at him, pleased. "That's all right,"
she said, dimpling at him. "My friends would kill for
a cookie and I'd kill for the white wine."

If at first David thought he'd walked into bedlam,
an hour later he was being fleeced by the inmates.
Unmercifully, and with great good humor.

Between hands Maurice said to Chelsea, "My God,
sweetie, the green stuff is turning black! Please cre-
mate it."

"Oh," Chelsea said, staring at the remains. "I guess Sarah forgot to add lemon. It keeps it from turning, you know."

"Come on, Maurice," Delbert said, "it still tastes good. All you've got to do is close your eyes."

Angelo belched. "More beer, Chels?"

Chelsea got to her feet and headed for the kitchen. David rose to stretch his legs and stare a moment at his dwindled pile of poker chips. He followed Chelsea into her kitchen.

"This place should be raided," he said. "When I saw that gleam in your eyes at the hospital I should have known I'd be out of my league."

"You'll notice who the big winner is, of course," Chelsea said blandly.

"Yeah. You've gotten about twenty dollars off me."

"So far," said Chelsea. She patted his arm and said in a lowered voice, "I wanted to tell you, you're doing great. My friends, well, they're very—"

"California. Laid back. Cutthroats."

"Only three words and you got right to the heart of the matter," she said, grinning. "And you're not even a writer. I am impressed."

He found himself smiling back. She looked cute; that was the only word to describe her at the moment. Her hair was mussed, her lipstick long gone and one earring was hanging precariously off her ear. He touched it.

"I hope they're not too expensive," he said.

"Oh, dear. I haven't quite gotten the knack yet, I don't think. I just got my ears pierced a little while ago."

"Want me to fix it for you?" David didn't wait for an answer. He turned her around and straightened the hoop. "You smell good," he said. His hand strayed to her bare neck.

That feels good, Chelsea realized, and for a moment she closed her eyes and enjoyed his fingers lightly stroking her skin.

"How 'bout we call a halt to the poker game? I don't want to write out any IOUs. I just bet Angelo would send someone to break my legs if I didn't pay up soon enough."

She felt his lips lightly touch her neck. That felt good, too, and she didn't move until his arm came around her and his hand caressed her stomach.

"I thought doctors were rich," she said.

"Probably not nearly so rich as writers," he said, his warm breath against her neck, "and your hours must be a hell of a lot saner than mine."

"So you want me to get rid of Maurice, Delbert and Angelo so we can neck?"

He grinned and ran his fingers through her thick soft hair. "Doesn't sound like a bad idea to me. If you really want to, I suppose I could force myself."

"None of my heros ever has to force himself," she said, slowly easing and turning to face him. "They're always eager."

"Last time I was eager, I got called a jerk."

"Actually," Chelsea said, smiling at the memory, "I called you a nerd, but maybe that was just to George. Don't look so hurt. After all, you called me a tease."

"Hey, Chels, where's my beer?" Angelo's voice carried extremely well.

"Why don't you give Angelo the rest of the six-pack and send him home happy?"

"Stop making out with that poor man, Chels!" Maurice yelled out.

"Ah, come on, Maurice," Delbert said. "He hasn't lost more than twenty bucks."

"Come on out, Chels," Maurice demanded in a louder voice. "We haven't checked this guy out enough yet."

"Yeah, he could be a mad rapist!" Angelo hooted.

"Hell," David said, "I'm never angry."

"My family," Chelsea said. She picked up Angelo's beer and walked out of the kitchen.

Lord, David thought, his eyes following her, she's got the cutest bottom.

Two hours later, and fifty dollars poorer, David stood beside Chelsea as she bid good-night to the poker gang and listened to each of them tell her what to do if he got fresh.

"You go for the lowest moving parts," Maurice said.

"Naw," said Angelo, "you bite his neck. Go right for the jugular."

When she closed the door she turned to face David and, for a moment, was taken aback at the look in his lovely eyes. Hero's eyes, she thought. Brilliant hazel. Very nice, all of him.

"Are you sorry you came?" she asked, not moving from the door.

"Will you loan me enough money for the toll back across the bridge?"

"You could always sell your body on the streets of Sausalito."

"You think I'd only get a dollar?"

"It's Friday night. The toll's two dollars."

"So that's what you think I'm worth, huh?"

"Your worth, doctor," she said, moving toward the wrecked living room, "is still in doubt."

He helped her clean up, grimacing at the black dregs of the guacamole. "That stuff *does* look disgusting. Next time use lemon," he said.

"Is Elliot teaching you how to cook?" she asked, arching an amused brow at him.

"Nope. I was just agreeing with Maurice."

Chelsea stacked the dishes in the sink, then fidgeted a bit putting leftovers into the refrigerator, aware that David was standing in the kitchen doorway watching her every move.

"I suppose," she said in a challenging voice, turning to face him, "that you want to neck now."

"You've got a cute bottom."

"I said neck, not bottom."

"I expect I'd make my way south, eventually."

She eyed him silently for a moment. "I suppose men think that if they've spent money on a woman the next step is bed. Let me remind you that you didn't *spend* a dime. You *lost* fifty bucks through lack of skill and cunning."

"You won about forty of that fifty dollars. Wouldn't you believe me if I swore I lost that money to you on purpose?"

"And that's the same thing? Do you know something, David? I don't even know if I like you."

"You know something, Chelsea? I don't know if I like you, either."

"Then why do you want to neck?"

"Because I think you're sexy. Don't you think I'm sexy, too?"

"Let me tell you something, Dr. Winter. I'm really very used to having the last word."

"Do your heroines always best your heroes verbally?"

She frowned at that. "Sometimes. Well, it depends. If the hero is a Mark I, my heroine gives him all sorts of grief verbally—" She broke off at his puzzled look. "A Mark I hero is the strong, macho, arrogant type. A Mark II hero is the witty, sexy, understanding, neat type."

"Which do you prefer?"

"Both."

"You don't want much, do you, lady?"

"We're talking about broad character types, David."

"That's what I tried to tell you last week. The stuff you write just isn't real, any of it. Your hero's supposed to be a woman's prince, isn't that right? The ultimate man with no flaws, a man who doesn't belch like Angelo, doesn't wag his finger like Maurice and is at least a foot taller than Delbert the jockey. You write fairy tales. Admit it."

"I will admit one thing," Chelsea said. "I write books to entertain. Escapist literature, if you wish. My readers are for the most part women. I ask you, if the very hassled woman of today takes time to read, does she want to read about the trials and tribulations of a real woman and her real husband—real people have to worry about bills, taxes, kids and probably worst of all commuting and the car breaking down. And real life extends to the bedroom. Does a real woman want to read about a man who's too tired to give her pleasure, or even worse, doesn't care. No, don't interrupt me! I did give you a chance. I write entertaining literature—yes, literature, David. It's not Proust or Stendhal. I have never wanted to write the great American novel. I just want to write what I enjoy reading, and I enjoy writing romance novels.''

"I suppose some women do need that sort of thing.''

"If you make it sound like a hefty dose of castor oil one more time, I'm going to smear the black guacamole on your face! Every damned novel, even your ridiculous Westerns, has romance in it. If there were no romance in life, this would be an awfully grim place. Don't you believe in romance? Didn't you experience it when you were going out with your ex-wife? You know, loss of appetite, all your thoughts of that one person—''

David held up his hands and sighed deeply. "How did this happen again? If I recall correctly, we've been through all this in fine detail before. All I wanted to do was neck.''

Chelsea, who'd learned from George how to expertly flick a towel, connected with David's thigh with a satisfying thwap. He yelped. She burst into laughter. "I've always said that if intelligent discussion fails, try pain.''

David straightened and, without a word, stalked toward her.

"David!''

She flicked him again with the towel, but only got his thick sweater. "Drat!'' She chose retreat and scurried around the kitchen table.

"It won't do you any good,'' David said. "You've now got a Mark I hero on your hands. The Mark II just expired quietly.''

"How much do you weigh?''

That stopped him for a moment. "One-eighty. Why?"

Chelsea inched nearer the doorway. "How tall are you, David?"

"Six-one or thereabouts. Why?"

"Well," she said, cocking her head, "you've got the basic ingredients for a Mark I." She dashed toward the open doorway. She yelled over her shoulder, "But I just bet you're slow!" She felt a strong arm circle her stomach, and then she was lifted and carried like a sack of avocados into the living room.

"Put me down, you jerk!"

"Is a jerk better than a nerd?"

"They're both equally repulsive!"

David sat down on the sofa and dragged Chelsea facedown over his thighs. "You've got the nicest bottom," he said, wistfully eyeing her.

"You already said that," Chelsea said, squirming to look up at him. "Parts is parts, David. Now let me up."

"Only if you promise to turn civilized and kiss me."

"All right," she said with no hesitation at all.

He was grinning when he turned her over. "Time to pay up, lady."

She was out of his arms and standing in front of him in an instant. "Your question was in reality two. When I said yes, I was answering only the first. Behold, a calm, civilized person."

He said nothing for a long moment, merely stared at her thoughtfully.

Chelsea said nervously, "I got you fair and square. Why don't you just admit it?"

"I'm trying to figure out what a Mark I hero would do in this situation. How 'bout if I throw you on the floor and tickle you until you plead for mercy?"

Chelsea shook her head. "No, that's a definite Mark II reaction. Much too lighthearted for a Mark I."

"Hmm, how 'bout if I grab you, fling you over my shoulder and toss you in the shower? Lots of cold water."

"That's just punishment with no real satisfaction for the hero. Nope, won't cut it."

"I think I've got it." David rose quickly, grabbed her hand and tossed her down onto the sofa. He eased down on top of her and pulled her hands above her head.

Chelsea didn't struggle. She felt the hard length of him on top of her, but he wasn't too heavy. It had been such a long time since she'd felt anything even remotely close to the kind of warmth he was so easily building in her. He leaned down and very gently touched his lips to hers. "I'm glad you've got a seven-foot sofa," he said against her mouth.

"I can't even think of a raunchy pun to go with that," she said. He kissed her again. "Are we necking yet?" she asked with a Transylvanian accent, and nibbled at his throat.

"No," he said slowly, "I don't think so." He paused a moment, then asked in a very intense voice, "Chelsea, do you ever get serious?"

"You have very white teeth."

"I know. Do you? I mean, do you ever respond to things in an appropriately serious manner?"

"Of course, but *things* rarely call for seriousness. You, on the other hand, probably go overboard with seriousness."

He said stiffly, "I certainly never laugh my way into a woman's bed."

"I wasn't aware that we were in anyone's bed. Besides, I doubt you could laugh your way into the shower!"

"We are, nearly," he snapped, pulling back from her, "and the shower is probably just where you belong."

Chelsea could only stare at him. "You mean you want heavy breathing and perhaps readings from Shakespeare's sonnets?"

"You're really quite immature," he said. "Quite immature." He swung off the sofa and rose, standing over her.

She still couldn't believe he was serious. "Shall I go dress in black?" she asked him, pulling her sweater back into its demure place. "Or perhaps I could just stuff a stocking in my mouth so I wouldn't lacerate your serious sensibilities with my immature humor."

He shoved his fingers through his thick hair. "Look, Chelsea, a sense of humor is all well and good, but when one is supposed to be serious...and involved, one doesn't want to make the other person feel that what he's doing is something to joke about."

"I don't believe you," she gasped. "Let me add that that convoluted sentence you just managed to string together is neither a Mark I or a Mark II thing to say. That's a stuffed-shirt-Eastern-pseudointellectual bit of garbage! No wonder your wife divorced you! You are the most full-of-it man I've ever met! And you can't even play poker decently!"

David felt more frustrated than angry. Damn it, she was a frivolous, silly California twit, with no pretense to anything but a cute butt, and her big mouth certainly took the attraction away from that attribute.

"And I am not immature," Chelsea said, scrambling up from the couch. "Just because I don't swoon all over you and sigh when you make your stupid male pronouncements, or moan with great seriousness when you kiss me—"

He shook his head, cutting her off sharply with, "Damn it, you drive me crazier, in a shorter amount of time, than any female I've ever known. Good night, Chelsea. Since you're trying to find a man, I'll be glad to keep my eyes open for you—but I doubt there's any male silly enough to endure your biting his throat like a vampire when he just wants—"

"Vampire! You idiot! If I were looking for a man, you, Dr. Great, wouldn't have gotten a second glance. And just wait a minute," she hollered after him. "I didn't finish my sentence! My sentence before this one!"

"Put it in your next novel! I'm sure you can think up a sufficiently revolting male villain to say it to."

"I'm going to kill you, George," Chelsea gritted, the slammed door rattling on its hinges. "I'd rather be bored than put up with that stuffed shirt."

Chapter 4

Damn it, Elliot, I even called her to apologize yesterday, and she had the nerve to hang up on me!"

"Then what did you do?" Elliot Mallory asked with great interest, although he knew full well what had transpired. Between taking care of Alex and visits from Chelsea, George was going nuts, and she had told him everything.

"I called her back. I asked her to go to dinner with me. And she told me she had a deadline and no time to *waste*! That fluff-headed woman needs a keeper!"

"I like the keeper part," Elliot said, unable to keep the grin off his face. "Usually, Sarah—her housekeeper—does a pretty decent job. What I don't understand, David, is why you're so heated up about all this. It sounds to me like you and Chelsea can't be together for five minutes without one of you going into a royal snit. This time you wanted to be serious and soulful and she wanted to play. Last time you treated

George and me to a marvelous battle-of-the-sexes act.
And, David, Chelsea isn't immature. She's very open
and giving and witty. It's just the way she is.''

"You're right. I was out of line, damn her eyes!''

Elliot blinked. He leaned back on his elbows and
stared out over the pool. The minute he'd seen David,
usually a morning swimmer, come in at one o'clock in
the afternoon, he had known he was in for it. Just the
night before he'd sworn to George that he wasn't going
to get involved anymore—"No, damn it, George,
that's it! Those two...keep your hands to yourself, no,
stop it, I won't change my mind''—but none of it had
done him any good. So much for swearing anything.

"She's so different, and I was very rude. What up-
sets me even more is that I don't know why I turned
into a Mr. Hyde. She's so lovely, so warm, and
I...well, I was an ass, damn it!''

"Did you ever hear about Chelsea's parents?'' Elliot asked, mentally praying for absolution himself
from the sin he was about to commit.

"No, why?''

"Well, if Chelsea acts a bit different sometimes, or
flippant, perhaps, you might consider her relationship with her parents. They're really quite rich, you
know. Her dad's a dentist, her mom a world traveler.
Chelsea's been alone a good deal of her life. I know
they don't help her financially, and I'm certain she's
much too proud to ask.'' Not one single lie, he
thought, congratulating himself. He was as good with
words as Chelsea. Maybe he should take up writing,
too. A medical thriller, maybe.

"But the condo in Sausalito. You know real estate
prices around here, Elliot.''

"She probably rents it, a special deal, I think George told me once. I don't know how she makes ends meet, poor girl." He managed a commiserating sigh.

"She won forty dollars off me at poker," David muttered.

"Good. Now she'll be able to afford groceries."

"She has a housekeeper!"

"I think Sarah gives her a break. Chelsea helped her husband get his mystery manuscript read at her publishing house."

"But what about her writing? Surely the kinds of books she writes sell, don't they?"

Elliot shrugged, saying only, "I've heard that publishing houses don't always pay as promptly as they should. Maybe she's got a problem with advances and holdbacks and stuff like that." Deception was a wearing experience, he thought. Chelsea, to the best of his knowledge, made more money than David, and as for her parents, they were utter screwballs, true, but they loved their only daughter to distraction. Why the hell was George so set on getting these two disparate specimens together?

He heard David say under his breath, "Then she'd never accept money from me. She's so little . . . I want her to eat."

"I've got an idea, David," Elliot said, rising and stretching. He felt pleasantly refreshed after his fifty laps. He also felt guilty for making David think Chelsea was a starving waif. "Why don't you wait a week, then give her another call?"

David looked alarmed, and Elliot said sharply, "She won't starve, David. Remember the forty dollars."

When Elliot dutifully related the conversation to his wife that evening over dinner she burst into laughter. "You, Elliot Mallory, are a born intriguer! Now all I've got to do is work on Chelsea. I've got a week, you say?"

"Yeah, if David doesn't break down and have groceries delivered to her house."

"That was really a nice touch," she said, marveling at his abilities. "Now you just leave the rest to me." She paused a moment, and he knew she was listening. "That, if my radar isn't off today, is the sound of your son demanding his dinner."

Elliot rose, hugged her against him and said, "Let's go marvel over the little devil together, okay?"

Mrs. Cambrey, their live-in nurse, appeared at that moment. She smiled. "You heard him, I guess?"

"Oh, yes, Anna. Why don't you go relax? Papa and I are going to do the honors."

"You two do too many of the honors now," Anna said. "I'm getting lazy and fat."

"It'll be my turn tomorrow," George said. "I'm going to pig out at a Mexican restaurant with a very dear, starving friend of mine."

George eyed Chelsea speculatively as she sipped her spritzer. It was a beautiful clear day, and they were lunching at Chelsea's favorite Mexican restaurant in Mill Valley.

George had waxed eloquent about her perfect son for a good fifteen minutes, giving Chelsea time to down one glass of white wine.

"I understand you're working under a deadline," George said, finally changing the subject as she crunched on a tortilla chip. "Hmm, yummy hot sauce."

Chelsea blinked. "You know I'm not. Where did you ever get that idea? I'm in the middle of the third book of the San Francisco trilogy."

"Oh, dear," George said, looking guilty, "I forgot. Forgive me, Chels. Have you decided what to order yet?"

"George," Chelsea said, bending her patented stare on her friend, "come clean."

"I think I'll try the macho burrito, with beef, not chicken. Come clean? It's just a silly misunderstanding, I'm sure. It's just that David told Elliot he wanted so much to apologize to you, and you told him you didn't have the time for him."

"So I lied," Chelsea said, shrugging elaborately. "I told you how obnoxious he was, George. Apologize, beans! That eastern uptight idiot probably doesn't know the meaning of the word."

"What do you think, Chels? Do refried beans come with the lunches?"

"George," Chelsea said in her most menacing voice. She had to put her flame on simmer because the waitress came up with a big smile and her pencil poised over her order pad.

"Another white wine for my friend, please," George called after her a moment later, as she left with their orders.

"Now," George said, "let me tell you something maybe you don't know about David." Unlike her husband, George was a firm believer in Machiavellian means. After all, she'd taken good care of her brother, Tod. Well, maybe not completely, but . . .

"I don't want to hear anything about that jerk!"

"It seems that what he said, the way he reacted to your joking around, was all the result of his first wife. It seems that once, when he had just finished a thirty-six-hour shift as an intern, he wasn't able to...well, perform. His wife laughed at him." *Dear heavens, I should be an author! Brilliant!*

If Chelsea were wearing socks, she would have been startled out of them, George thought. Indeed, she seemed so upset that it didn't occur to her to think it unlikely that any man would admit to nonperformance, much less to a woman laughing at him about it.

"But...but I wasn't laughing at him! How could he have thought that? We were joking around, talking about necking and Mark I and Mark II heroes, and we ended up on the sofa. All I did was nibble on his neck—maybe not all that funny, but I was kind of nervous. I just did a tiny bit of my Dracula routine. George, for heaven's sake, I'm not used to lying around with a man on top of me."

I wasn't, either, until Elliot. She said in her most consoling voice—at least she hoped it was consoling—"Poor David, he's so lonely, you know. You must realize that he misses his kids something awful, and he works so hard. Sometimes eighteen hours a day, Elliot told me."

Chelsea sat back in her chair, her white wine in one hand, her chin propped up on the other. "You know, he did very well with my crazy friends that night. And he was amusing, and funny. I just never thought that...well..."

"Exactly," said George. "Ah, here's my macho burrito!"

Chelsea stared down at her nacho plate, but for one of the few times in her twenty-eight years she didn't have any appetite for her beloved Mexican food. "I've been a jerk," she said. "His wife *laughed* at him?"

"So sad," George said, shaking her head as she cut enthusiastically into her burrito.

Chelsea said in a glum voice, "I'll just bet he doesn't call me again."

"Well," George said brightly, "perhaps it's just as well. Maybe it's true that opposites don't attract, or shouldn't, in any case. Hand me the hot sauce, please, Chels."

Chelsea frowned at her, wondering how she could be so utterly insensitive. They weren't really opposites, after all.

"Hello. Chelsea?"

She gripped the phone tightly. "Yes. David?"

"Yes. I was wondering if maybe you were finished with your deadline."

"As a matter of fact I sent the manuscript off just this morning," she said with great untruth. "How are you, David?"

David blinked at the phone. He heard a man shouting at an intern in the emergency room and quickly kicked the door to the small lunchroom shut with his foot. She sounded happy to hear from him. "I, uh, would you like to have dinner with me? Now that you're not under any more pressure from your publisher."

"When?"

"Uh, well, how about tomorrow night? Do you have a favorite place?"

Elsa opened the door at that moment. "Dr. Winter, we've got a motorcycle accident."

"I'll be right there." To Chelsea, he said quickly, "Emergency, I'm sorry. I'll pick you up at seven o'clock, all right?"

"That would be grand," Chelsea said, and smiled, a sweet, tender, understanding smile, as she gently replaced the receiver. Poor man, she thought, looking with a bemused smile at the now silent phone. She'd been insensitive to him with all her joking around. But she had been nervous. She sighed. To be honest with herself, for once, her thinking continued on a rueful smile, she hadn't had that much experience with men, and the little experience she'd had, had left her lukewarm, if not cold. Only heroines in her novels enjoyed sex. Only heroes, spun from her optimistic imagination, were perfect lovers. And how was she to deal with a man whose wife had laughed at him when he couldn't "perform," as George had put it? She shuddered. Even her heroines—although never faced with such a circumstance—certainly wouldn't laugh! No, her heroines would be loving and caring and full of tender concern.

Oh, hell! Reality simply wasn't like what went on in her novels. David was right about that. But for that matter, reality wasn't what was portrayed in his damned Westerns. Stupid, pigheaded man!

Chelsea rose and walked out the front door, yelling back to Sarah, who was making a salad, that she was going for a walk. She crossed Bridgeway and walked down the road that led to the sailboat docks on Richardson Bay. San Francisco and Marin were the most beautiful spots in the United States, she decided. The day was perfectly clear, and when she walked out on the farthest dock she could see Alcatraz and San Francisco in all their glory. She wondered where David's sailboat was berthed.

After a few moments of indulging in the scenery Chelsea began to plot, something as natural to her as breathing. Why not, she thought, consider writing a follow-up trilogy using the children of her current heroes and heroines? She wasn't usually big on sequels because of all their pitfalls—such as heroines now in their forties or fifties still with eighteen-inch waists—but it was something to think about. She remembered how the trilogy had gotten started, all from the fan mail she'd received for one novel, touting the hero's brother. And he, bless his heart, was now the hero in the first of the trilogy.

Chelsea continued wandering, thinking about the young heroine in her current novel. Her name was Juliana—Jules, for short—and she was in for a tough time. Now what should I do once I have her married to the hero? How will he act toward her? Paternal? Benevolent? Yes, of course, that's obvious, but next she . . .

The blast of a car horn brought her out of her plotting fog.

"Watch where you're going, lady!"

She hadn't realized that she'd stepped off the curb into the oncoming traffic. She shouted out a "Sorry!" and scurried across the street. I know. She'll want her husband to love her, but doesn't know how to go about it. Then Byrony and Brent will get into the act, along with Chauncey and Delaney. Then there's the obsession Wilkes has with her. Ah, endless opportunities. . . .

She stretched out on a blanket in her front yard and plotted away the afternoon.

"You look gorgeous," David said smiling down at Chelsea the following evening precisely at seven o'clock. "You haven't lost any weight, have you?"

She cocked her head. "That's always the least of my problems," she said. "How are you, David? Are you dreadfully tired?"

"No, not really. Today wasn't particularly slow, but it wasn't a madhouse, either."

She patted his arm. "I'm glad. You don't want to wear yourself out. You look very fine. I don't think we should waste your finery on the place I was thinking of. Have you ever been to the Alta Mira?"

He hadn't, and was duly impressed by the panoramic view from the hotel dining room windows.

David ordered a very expensive Chablis, looking briefly toward Chelsea to see if she approved. She did, and beamed at him.

Lord, he thought, forcing his eyes down to the ornate menu, she looked lovely tonight. He liked the clingy dress, but wondered how she managed to get around without stumbling and killing herself on the three-inch high heels she was wearing. Maybe, he thought, she wanted to come up to his chin. Her black hair was fluffy and soft-looking and framed her pixie face adorably.

"And the seafood salads are delicious," Chelsea said after a while. He'd had enough time to study the menu through three times!

David set down the menu and smiled at her. "Why don't you order for me? I'm a sucker for seafood, particularly shrimp or crab. Ah, and here's the wine.

Why don't you taste it? You're the one with the expert taste buds."

Chelsea tasted, approved and ordered for both of them. She sat back in her chair, feeling suddenly shy. She swallowed, then began her tour guide rundown on the sights they could see from their table.

"You keep your fingernails short. I like that," he said when she'd finally ground to a halt with Strawberry Point, just across Richardson Bay from them.

"Oh," Chelsea said, curling her fingers under. She hadn't filed her nails in an age. "Well, it's hard to type with long nails."

"It would be pretty hard on my patients if I didn't keep mine short, too," he said.

"I don't know," she said thoughtfully, a dimple appearing on her left cheek. "If the patient were particularly obnoxious, you could slip just a bit."

He thought of just such a particularly obnoxious man who'd come into the emergency room yesterday with bruised knuckles from a fight and complained because he'd had to wait for thirty minutes. He took another sip of wine, then said cautiously, "I understand that in your profession, your money doesn't come to you regularly."

"That's right," Chelsea agreed. "I call it a bolus of bucks when it does arrive."

"Bolus? Do you know what a bolus is?"

"Sure, it's a big shot of something you give to a patient who needs the something very quickly."

"You got that from Elliot, right?"

"Yep. I'll have to tell George that Elliot has indeed been good for something."

He didn't know what to make of that, but he was tenacious and wasn't to be sidetracked. "Are you expecting a bolus of bucks soon?"

"Why?" She cocked her head questioningly. "Do you need a loan?"

Her voice was teasing, but David, so concerned that she was only eating a salad for dinner, didn't catch it. "No. Wouldn't you like a steak or something more substantial to go with the salad?"

"You, David, haven't yet seen the Alta Mira salads! It's the kind of serving you have to take home and eat for three days."

Oh, God, that was why she'd ordered the salad. He closed his eyes for a moment, aware that he had to tread very carefully.

"When will you get to see your kids?" Chelsea asked, wanting to take his hand, perhaps to comfort him. He didn't look particularly miserable, as George had said he was, but some people hid their feelings very well. Her heroes especially, at least the Mark Is.

"My kids? At Christmas. They'll be coming out from Boston for a couple of weeks. Then, with any luck at all, they'll come out here again during the spring. Would you like a slice of bread, Chelsea? With butter? Here's some delicious-looking strawberry jam."

She shook her head. "Why don't you have some? It's really wonderful. I bet you really miss them."

"Yeah, I do. Why don't I order us some soup?"

"David, I'm not all that hungry."

"All right," he said quickly, not wanting her to become suspicious. "You told me you were an only child. That must have been tough."

"Tough? Not really, I've got a couple of zany parents. Didn't I tell you about them?"

He tried to remember, but only Elliot's words were clear in his mind. "No, not much, at any rate. What makes you say they're zany?"

Chelsea laughed, a clear, sweet sound. "Actually, I think the word was invented for them." She saw that he wanted to hear more and set out to making it amusing. "My dad, if you don't recall, is a dentist. Imagine if you can a man in his early fifties, as tanned as any surfer, with a gold chain around his neck. He's a health food freak and jogs five miles a day. All this, you understand, while my mother is either packing or unpacking for or from a trip to the Lord knows where. How about your folks? Are they a bit zany or... ultraconservative?"

"The latter," he said. She was so brave, he thought, no bitterness at all in her voice when she spoke of her parents. He couldn't help it. He pictured a lonely little girl—who somehow managed in his mind to have a cute bottom—who escaped her miserable existence in fantasy. "Is that why you started writing?" he asked abruptly.

Chelsea blinked and took another drink of wine. "Writing? I started writing because, like many writers I know, I'm also a voracious reader, and one day I threw the novel I was reading across the room and said I could do better. That's how I started writing."

"Oh." So she'd read a lot to escape her loneliness. He pictured a lonely little girl curled up in a corner with books piled around her, thick glasses on her nose....

"Do you wear glasses for reading?"

His mental leaps were most odd, but Chelsea didn't mind. She thought again that for a very lonely, over-worked man, he was extremely charming. She had a fleeting memory of him lying on top of her on the sofa and felt a bit of warmth at the thought. Oh, well, she thought, it wouldn't have continued even if he hadn't turned weird on her. She probably would have frozen up on him and kicked him out of her condo. She sighed.

"Chelsea, do you wear glasses for reading?" he repeated, wondering at the myriad expressions that had flitted across her expressive face. Oh, Lord, maybe she couldn't afford glasses. Just maybe...

"No, I've got perfect vision, just like my dad. Old Eagle Eye, I call him."

Thank God, he thought.

"Do you wear reading glasses—or operating glasses, as the case may be?"

He shook his head. "You're very small," he said abruptly.

That brought forth a merry laugh, which was cut off with the arrival of their waiter, carrying two heaped plates.

"Do you think this will fill in all the cracks, doctor?"

"Most impressive," David said. Lots of shrimp, he thought. That was good.

He took a bite and nodded in approval. "How tall are you, Chelsea?"

"I'm afraid that, like the pink stuff on the plate, I'm also something of a shrimp. Five foot two and a half. My dad used to have me do stretching exercises, complained like mad that it was all my mother's fault, bad genes and all that."

Had Chelsea but known it, she was attaining near saintlike stature in David's eyes for her lighthearted treatment of what must have been an utterly miserable childhood. He saw that she wasn't eating and began talking, to give her time to attack her meal.

"And then there was this guy who came into the emergency room at Mass General with appendicitis. Now that's okay, but he also had a huge tattoo on his belly, in vivid color, of a lady on her back, her legs twined around his navel."

"You're putting me on!" Chelsea nearly choked on her wine. "Please tell me you took a picture?"

"Nope, but the intern who shaved him before the operation was very careful to leave lots of hair on the naked lady's feet. The surgical team nearly broke up."

Chelsea had a faraway look in her eyes, and the dimple was playing on her cheek.

"What are you thinking?"

"Oh, I was thinking about putting a scene in a book like that. The guy's name could be Jonathan, and he could be a minister, say, who'd suffered stomach pains for a long time because he was afraid that people would report his tattoo to the press and he'd be laughed at. You see, some friends talked him into the tattoo when he was very young and in the navy. Poor man. I suppose he'll survive and the surgeon, someone like you, David, would keep mum about it."

David stared at her for a long moment. "You're something else, you know that?"

"Not really," Chelsea said quickly, a bit embarrassed. "Did you like the salad? Would you like dessert? It's really quite obscene here, you know."

"Obscene? That sounds interesting. No, nothing for me. But you'd like something, wouldn't you, Chelsea?"

He'd handled it wrong, he thought when she shook her head. If he'd ordered something, maybe she would have, too. He could at least have talked her into taking bites of his. Well, next time he'd be brighter.

He had a sudden inspiration. "Let's stop and get some cookies, all right?"

"You're determined to add dignity to my derriere, aren't you?"

He gave her a beatific smile.

Chapter 5

Why are you so nervous, you silly twit? Chelsea grinned at her silent castigation. She loved to talk historical to herself. But she was nervous, she supposed, perhaps because David might turn weird on her again. Well, she decided, this time I will act very serious.

To her surprise, when they reached her condo he gently touched his hands to her arms, leaned down and very lightly kissed her. He didn't even give her a chance to show him the temporary depths of her seriousness.

"I'll speak to you soon, Chelsea. Thanks for a great evening." He waved once and disappeared into his car, a black Lancia named Nancy. The car's license plate was NANCY W. When she'd kidded him about having a vanity plate on the way back to her condo, he'd said that even Easterners occasionally had bouts of whimsy.

"Most odd," Chelsea said, walking into her living room a few moments later. She really wouldn't have minded a bit more than that sterile kiss. She jumped at the sound of the doorbell.

"Yes?" she asked, opening the door without unfastening the chain.

"It's David. You forgot your doggie bag."

Chelsea blinked, utterly bewildered. Was that an odd come-on? No, it couldn't be. He was serious. It hadn't been her idea in the first place to trot the rest of her salad home. Wilted lettuce wasn't her idea of gourmet dining. Oh, well, since he had been nice enough to bring it back ... She opened the door, and David, smiling down at her, thrust the doggie bag into her hand. "Sleep well," he said, and was gone again.

"Most extraordinarily odd," she said, and tossed the doggie bag into the trash compactor. "Well, I've never known a man from Boston before. Maybe they're all like he is. Odd and cute, and an occasional touch of whimsy."

By the time she eased into bed an hour later she'd convinced herself that he was very tired—after all those long hours at the hospital—and needed his rest.

Next time, she thought, burrowing her head into her pillow, she'd get him to kiss her a bit more. An experiment.

To her surprise, the next morning she was yanked from the 1850s by the ringing phone beside her desk. Usually her agent, editor and friends didn't call her until afternoon, the hours from eight o'clock in the morning until noon being sacred. "Yes?"

"Chelsea? David."

She immediately shifted from her standoffish voice. "Oh, hello. How are you? Just a second, let me turn off my computer."

David heard some shuffling about, then her voice again. "Okay."

"Are you busy tonight?"

"Well, I—"

"I apologize for calling you so late, but I just managed to arrange coverage."

"That's all right," she assured him. "No, I'm not busy. How about I buy you dinner this evening? I know this great place and—"

There was dead silence on the line.

"David?"

He was thinking furiously. The last thing he wanted was for her to spend her meager supply of money on his dinner! "Yes, I'm here. Actually, I wanted to invite you to my apartment—I'll cook you dinner."

"I didn't think you cooked."

"I'm a quick study, don't you remember? Don't worry, I won't poison you."

And so it was that Chelsea, dressed casually in jeans, a pullover and new dangly earrings, drove into the city that evening. *He probably invited me to his apartment so he could make out,* she thought, cynical and interested all at the same time. *But what was wrong with my apartment? Unanswerable.*

David lived on Telegraph Hill near Coit Tower, and it took Chelsea thirty minutes to find a parking place. His apartment was more or less a penthouse in a four-flat building. The view was an unbelievable panorama of the Bay and the city. He was cooking the most enormous steaks she'd ever seen out on the covered deck.

"Are you sure you don't need to borrow some money from me?" she asked in a teasing voice after a brief tour of the luxurious apartment. "This is quite a setup, doctor. I'm beginning to think that I'm in the wrong profession."

He nodded and smiled and showed her his study.

"Ah, just look at all those Westerns! And is that Proust tucked back in there? But your collection is lacking, David. Tell you what, I'll autograph some of my books for you. Add some taste and color to your shelves."

"I'd like that. But better, let me go buy some. You do get royalties, don't you?"

"About thirty-two cents a book. I foresee earning another dollar off you."

Better than nothing, he thought. He didn't notice the designer jeans she was wearing, which cost a good thirty dollars a leg.

When they sat down at David's kitchen table a little while later David had his fingers crossed. Elliot had told him how long to cook the steak, what vegetable to buy and how long to keep it in the microwave, and what dressing to use on the salad. He'd also bought a huge bottle of white wine, her favorite Chablis, despite the red meat dinner.

"This is decadent," Chelsea said, eyeing the huge piled plate in front of her.

"I hope you like everything," David said.

She looked him straight in the eye. "Yes, I do. Like everything, that is," she added, giving him an impish smile. He looked better than the dinner, she thought. His hair was tousled from his stint of cooking the steaks on the windy deck. He was wearing a white shirt, rolled up to his elbows, with jeans. A nice combination, she decided. She liked the hint of curling hair she saw on his chest.

"Chelsea, eat," David said.

She took a bite of steak and made approving noises.

"Are you dreadfully tired, David?" she asked after managing five bites of steak. She wasn't much of a red meat lover, but he looked so apprehensive she vowed to consume every bit.

"Tired?" He blinked at that. "No, why would you ask?"

"You work such long hours. Elliot said something about eighteen hours a day."

Elliot had said that? Why, for God's sake? He did, sometimes, but all of them did. But Chelsea was regarding him with such sweet concern that he hesitated to tell her the truth. He temporized. "Well, occasionally, but not all that often, really. Just sometimes."

"Ah, very clear, Doctor. I, on the other hand, lead such a lazy life that I many times feel guilty."

"But your writing—"

"I write about five hours a day, usually. I find that my creative brain cells give out at about one in the afternoon. Then I'm as free as the proverbial bird."

"Aren't you ever lonely, Chelsea?"

"Sometimes," she agreed, forking down some quite well-prepared green beans. "But you see, I have a small group of friends, and I have all my characters, and Lord knows my poor brain is working all the time on their problems."

"Friends' and characters' problems?"

"Primarily just my characters' problems. My friends do very well without my advice. I do have to watch myself with the plotting. It puts me in something of a fog. I nearly bit the bullet the other day crossing the street without my brain being there with my body."

He looked alarmed. "You must be careful about that."

"I was just joking, David. Not to worry."

"More wine?"

"Certainly," she said, her eyes sparkling. "Sometimes I think I'm a wino in the making."

"How much do you drink?"

He'd asked in his professional doctor's voice, and Chelsea began to laugh. "Now, David, enough of that. Next thing I know, you'll be sending me a bill for professional care."

"Oh, no, I promise."

He was treating her with kid gloves, she realized suddenly. Most odd, was her first thought. And on their last date he'd asked so many questions about her parents and her income. As if she were a mental patient or something. Disconcerting.

She shoved her plate back. "No more, not another bite, you've stuffed me royally."

He started to urge her to eat more, then bit his tongue. He said easily, "I'll make you up a doggie bag, just like a restaurant."

Warmed over steak? Surely he must be kidding.

But she only smiled. "Why don't you show me some photos of your kids? I'd love to see them. Do they look like you?"

"Okay, and yes, Taylor does."

How, David wondered some fifteen minutes later, could he have ever believed her obnoxious or fluff headed? She was warm, caring and showed such interest in his children that he was a bit dazed. In fact, his thinking continued as he rifled through snapshots of a vacation in the Bahamas three years before, she was treating him almost too warmly, as if he were a shell-shocked soldier sent home from the battlefield. A bit bizarre.

As for Chelsea, she was gazing with avid interest at several photos of David in a swimsuit, sprawled on the white sand in Nassau. And the one of him standing, looking every bit as gorgeous as any of her heroes.... She particularly liked the sprinkling of hair on his chest, and the traditional thinner line of hair to his belly.

"Very nice," she managed, her voice a bit thin.

"What? Oh, the pictures? The Bahamas, as I said."

"No, you. Your photos are very nice. You're an athlete, I suppose."

"I jog and swim," David said. "And I try not to pig out too often."

"It shows. One thing that drives me crazy is novels where the hero is a businessman who probably sits on his derriere ten hours a day and has the most perfect body imaginable. I simply can't imagine how he could get such a bod, much less keep it." She added, beaming at him, "At least yours is justified."

He groaned. "Not back to Mark I and Mark II, are we?"

"No," Chelsea said firmly. "I don't want you to think I'm frivolous again."

"Look," David said, sliding his long fingers through his hair, "I really am sorry about that. I don't know what got into me."

You remembered your wife laughing at you for being impotent.

"And I have something of a snap temper, I suppose. Are we both forgiven?"

He nodded.

"Behold a very serious woman."

"Please, Chelsea, I didn't mean, that is...do whatever you want to."

"Well, I can't drink any more wine because I've got to drive home in a little while." She paused, seeing his eyes cloud at her words. Poor David, he was so lonely. "Do you like to dance?" she asked abruptly.

"As a matter of fact I do. I'm really quite good."

"Are you now?" She slanted him a challenging look.

"Yes, ma'am. Let's go to Union Street. There's a great place there, but noisy."

"You're on!"

They had a great time until David got beeped. "Damn," he said. Chelsea, fearing the worst, followed him as he immediately went to a phone and made a call.

"Damn," she heard him say again, and then he listened. "I'll be right there. Call Dr. Braidson and tell her what's happened. Ask her to come in right away." He set the phone down, looking at it for a moment as if it were an alien instrument. Why tonight? he was thinking.

He gave her a rueful look. "I'm sorry, but there's an emergency, and my coverage just collapsed under a heap of bodies."

"No problem. I can take a taxi back to my car."

He looked indecisive for a moment. "I'm afraid I've got to let you, but I don't want to, Chelsea. Look, can I see you this weekend? Maybe Saturday? We could go sailing if the weather's nice."

"Fine," Chelsea said, and looked at his mouth.

He quickly leaned down and kissed her lightly. He stroked his long fingers over her jaw, kissed the tip of her nose and left.

"You're not a bad dancer," she called after him. He turned briefly and smiled.

"You ain't, either, kiddo!"

The morning was sunny and warm a week before Thanksgiving, but Chelsea, as a native Californian, expected nothing else. She dropped down to retie the lace on her sneaker, then stood up, stretched a bit and breathed in the wonderful smell of the eucalyptus trees all around her in Golden Gate Park. She wished George could have been with her today, but Georgina, the cover girl, was off making a commercial in Boston, the first since Alex's birth, and wasn't due back until this evening. Okay, lazy buns, she told herself, let's go!

Chelsea enjoyed jogging. She wasn't as disciplined as George, nor did she have as much endurance, but she could go a couple of miles in the park before collapsing in a heap.

A few moments later her feet were working on maintaining a smooth pace and her brain was solidly in 1854 in San Francisco—before the park was even here, she realized with a smile. Back then she'd have been running on sand dunes and breathing in gritty sand.

Now, her plotting voice said, our hero Michael— nickname, Saint. Love it. I've got to find a couple of books on what doctors knew and did back then, and oh, yes, I've already established him as a great story-teller, so there's no reason not to use funny tidbits about medical history, if I can find them. And as for

Jules, it's neat that she's from Maui, a great place then, with all the whalers and—

Chelsea heard the strangled whoosh of a motor right behind her, pulled herself back to the present and turned quickly. But it was too late. A guy was fighting with a moped, and losing. How weird-looking it was, she thought blankly in that split second, with all those tools and things tied to the bars.

The moped slammed into her, and she felt something sharp and cold against her stomach. The force of it sent her hurtling onto her back into a clump of azaleas. Her head struck a rock, and she gasped, a small, soft sound.

Chelsea came to her senses, aware that she was moving and that there was a loud noise dinning in her ears.

"Take it easy," a soothing voice said, and she felt a gentle hand on her shoulder. "Just lie still."

"Where am I?"

"In an ambulance. We'll be at the hospital in just a moment."

"What happened?" Her voice sounded odd, high and thin, almost like a child's. The siren made her head ache abominably.

"A moped hit you and knocked you down. I think the damned fool is stoned."

"My stomach," she gasped suddenly, trying to hug her arms about her and draw up her legs, but she felt hands holding her, and the soothing voice continued telling her to lie still.

It isn't *your* stomach that's on fire, she wanted to shout to that voice, but she didn't. She hurt too badly.

Her mind latched onto her doctor in 1854, Saint. But at the moment she couldn't find the humor in it. "I was on the side of the road, not in anyone's way," she said. Then her mind fizzled out, the pain damping everything.

"I know," the voice said, "just hang on."

What was that about the moped being stoned?

She moaned again, feeling tears sting her eyes.

Suddenly the movement stopped, and she was aware of being flat on her back on some sort of moving table. There were voices and faces peering down at her.

"In here," a woman's clear voice said.

The table stopped, and there was a man leaning over her. "Do you understand me, Miss?"

She licked her lower lip. "Yes," she said.

"Where does it hurt?"

"My stomach."

The face was gone, and suddenly she felt her clothes being pulled off.

"What the hell! Chelsea!"

It was David's voice, blank with surprise. He was leaning over her now, and the other man was gone. "What happened to you?"

"Stoned," she managed. "Moped."

She heard the first man tell him about her stomach.

Suddenly she felt cool air on her chest. Dear God, they were stripping her in front of David. She yelled, "Stop it! Don't you dare take my clothes!"

"Chelsea—" David's voice was low, soothing, immensely professional, and she hated it "—I've got to examine you, and I can't do it with your clothes on. Now, just hold still and relax. All right?"

"No!" She tried to get up, but strong hands were on her shoulders, pressing her down. "Get away from me!"

"I won't hurt you," David said, holding her as gently as he could. Damn it, he had to get her calmed down. "Please, Chelsea, hold still!"

She was panting, the pain jabbing at her, making her want to yell. "Get out, David! You're not going to see me with no clothes on! Get out!"

There were several moments of pandemonium.

David drew a sharp breath. He leaned over her and took her face between his hands. "Listen to me!" He held her head until her eyes focused on his face. "No more of this damned nonsense, do you hear me? I am a doctor and you are now a patient and you're hurt. If you don't hold still, I'm going to belt you. You got that, Chelsea?"

"I don't want you to," Chelsea said.

"I don't give a damn. Now, will you hold still and try to act like a reasonable adult?"

"I hate you."

"Good, just hold still and try to cooperate."

Oh, Lord, David thought, finally releasing her. "Your belly hurts?"

"Yes."

"I'm going to check it out now. Don't move!"

David straightened and took a needle from Elsa, who was standing beside him. "Chelsea, you're going to feel a little prick. I'm just taking some blood."

She didn't really feel anything, just a bit of odd pressure. "My stomach," she whispered. "It feels numb and hot at the same time."

"I know. Just hold still." She heard him say something about crossing and typing, and something else about a crit.

Chelsea felt her shorts and panties being dragged over her hips and down her legs. Her sneakers made a silly thumping noise when they hit the floor. She closed her eyes, feeling more humiliated and embarrassed than she ever had in her entire life. And she hurt.

She gritted out, "The jerk was stoned! I was plotting, David, but it wasn't my fault. I was out of the way!"

"I know. Don't worry now." David saw the pool of blood on her belly and motioned quickly to Elsa. Gently he swabbed away the blood. He saw the puncture mark immediately. There had been something sharp on the moped and it had gone into her just as if she'd been stabbed. But how deep? That was the important question.

"Chelsea," he asked, "does this hurt?"

"Yes," she whispered, flinching away from his fingers.

She heard a woman's voice saying crisply, "Blood pressure 110/80, pulse 145."

She saw David's head very close to her stomach. "Relax, Chelsea," he said, not looking at her. As gently as he could he probed the wound, trying to find the base. He hoped nothing vital had been penetrated. He didn't think so, but he wasn't certain. He said to the nurse, "Get an IV going now."

His mind was sorting through options as he straightened and took out his stethoscope. He listened to her heart and lungs. Suddenly he heard her moan, and he flinched.

"Chelsea," he said, taking her face between his hands again, "something on the moped stabbed you. What we've got to do, now, is an exploratory laparotomy. I can't take the risk that something vital wasn't penetrated. In a moment I'll have you sign some papers. Then I'll give you a shot and there won't be any more pain. All right?"

"It hurts," Chelsea said. "So does my wretched head."

"I imagine it does. But you're going to be just fine, I promise. Now hold still, just another quick prick." He got the IV going and ordered antibiotics.

"I don't like this at all," Chelsea said, trying very hard not to sob. "I don't want you looking at me!"

"Now I'm just going to look at your head." She felt a sheet being pulled over her. It had taken them long enough, she thought angrily. "How many fingers, Chelsea?"

"Four."

"Good, now follow my finger."

She did. He started probing, and she tried to jerk away when he found the small lump behind her left ear. "Hold still," he said sharply. She felt him strike her lightly with something, and one elbow jumped, then the other. "Tell me if you feel this," he said.

"Ouch!"

David took the needle he'd been lightly pricking against her legs and gently scratched it up the bottom of her bare foot. "Feel that?"

"Yes."

He looked closely into her eyes with a silly-looking instrument. He said while he looked, "I don't think there's any doubt that you know who you are and who

I am. Your brain is intact. Everything looks good here.''

"I don't like lying here like a piece of meat," she said.

"I wouldn't, either. Now I've got to examine the rest of you. Just relax."

He gently turned her onto her stomach, and the pain in her stomach intensified. She stuffed her fist into her mouth.

David checked every inch of her back, bottom and legs. No other puncture wounds, no bruises. He stroked his hands over her ribs. "Any pain?"

She shook her head, not speaking.

He shifted her onto her back again and pulled the sheet over her. Her face was white with pain. He knew he was going to operate, and he also knew he should wait for the anesthesiologist, but he didn't wait. He told Elsa in a low voice to bring morphine.

Chelsea's eyes were closed, and her lashes only flickered slightly when he asked, "There's no pain anywhere but your belly?"

She managed to gasp out, "It's just my rotten stomach!"

"Okay, now I'm going to raise you a bit. Here's a pen. Sign right here."

"What is it? My will? I'm leaving you all my money?"

"No, you're giving me permission to do a laparotomy. That's all."

She wanted to ask what a laparotomy was, but she felt a sharp bolt of pain in her stomach and couldn't think straight. She signed the paper.

"Good," David said. He injected the morphine into her IV line and checked again to see that the tape holding the needle in her arm was secure.

"You're a damned lecher," she gritted out. "Don't you dare pull that sheet down again."

She thought she heard some laughter, but wasn't certain. David was leaning over her again. "Now just breathe normally. You're not going out yet, but the pain is going to all but go away. Then I'm going to take some very pretty pictures of your insides. Then the OR."

What the devil was the OR? she wondered vaguely. Operating room. "No!" she yelled, trying desperately to sit up. Everything was spinning. David's face flickered in and out.

"You look ridiculous in that dumb white coat," she said; then she felt incapable of doing or saying anything else.

She felt insensible, her brain like mush, but at least the pain was only a dull throbbing.

David was saying, "Get me Dr. Madson. I want him to do the surgery."

He took Chelsea's hand in his, and for the first time since he'd seen her sprawled on the gurney he smiled. "You're going to be all right, Chels. And when you wake up you won't be able to yell at me for operating on you." Dr. Madson was the finest abdominal surgeon on staff. He shook his head. She'd actually called him a lecher!

He held her hand while Dr. Corning, the anesthesiologist, asked her questions.

"What do you mean, do I take any drugs?" she asked, her voice slurred and slow. "Ask that idiot on the moped."

"Chelsea, are you on any antibiotics, prescribed stuff like that?"

"No," she said, "not even birth control pills."

Thorpe Corning smiled at David and said suavely, "Something for you to take care of, David. Now, Miss Lattimer, any allergies? Like to penicillin?"

"No, and please stop. I don't do anything except drink white wine."

"All right," Thorpe said, "now here's what's going to happen." Neither doctor was certain that she heard or understood.

"Take good care of her, Thorpe," David said.

"I always do, my man," Dr. Corning said, grinning as he rose. "And since she's a special interest, I'll sing to her while she's going under. I gather that's why you're not doing the surgery?"

"You got it," David said. "Besides, Dennis does pretty stitching."

Chelsea was aware of white, an endless expanse of white. She frowned, then gasped aloud at the throbbing pain in her stomach.

She heard a voice, a very gentle, firm voice, telling her to hold still.

Then David was saying insistently, "Chelsea. Open your eyes."

She could manage that, just barely. He was blurred at first, but she kept blinking until he was in focus.

David looked down at her, trying to smooth the lines of worry from his forehead. After all, the surgery had gone well. She just looked so small and lost, swathed in the white hospital gown, her face nearly as white as the sheets. Her black hair was tousled, her lips pale, devoid of her usual peach lipstick. She looked vulnerable, helpless, and he wished he could magically change this day into tomorrow. Even with painkiller, she would feel like the pits for a good eight more hours. He saw her bite her lower lip. He gently picked up her hand and held it.

"Chelsea," he said, "I know you hurt, but try not to fight it, all right? Just take shallow breaths. Abdominal surgery isn't pleasant, but the pain won't last all that long. I'll give you something for it in a little while."

"What are you doing here?" she asked, his words going through and over her head. She felt muddled and heavy and stupid. "I'm in bed, but my bedroom isn't white like this. I didn't invite you to spend the night, did I?"

"Not this time, no. You're in the hospital. Do you remember the moped?"

"I'm not stupid or senile." She flinched, remembering that odd sharp pain in her stomach. Now she remembered everything.

She heard him chuckle.

"You told me it wouldn't hurt anymore. What's wrong?"

He heard the fear in her voice and repeated what he'd already said. "You've had surgery. You were very lucky. The wound didn't penetrate anything important. You're going to be up and about in another week."

Surgery! Someone had cut her open! David!

But she couldn't work up the outrage to tell him that he'd had no right—no right at all—to cut her open; she felt too crummy. She swallowed the gasps of pain that threatened to erupt from her throat and turned her face away on the very hard pillow.

David straightened, releasing her hand. Dennis Madson had done a fine job. The incision was small, the stitches set beautifully, and he'd only given David an understanding smile when he'd said he didn't want to assist. David had paced the waiting room like an expectant father during the entire surgery, too scared out of his wits and much too worried to assist Dennis. It was only when it was over that Dennis had showed him the results.

He wished he could find something to say, but he couldn't. He knew she was upset, hurting and confused. He smoothed some black curls away from her forehead again, his touch featherlight. He thanked the good Lord that he'd been there in the emergency room to take care of her.

"You silly woman," he said very softly, smiling crookedly as he remembered her shouting at him, "You lecher!" He knew stories were already buzzing around the emergency room about Dr. Winter's lady friend coming in and yelling at him for taking off her clothes. He wondered how long he would have to endure the inevitable razzing.

Seeing that her face was white with pain, he shaved the time by thirty minutes. He said nothing to her, merely injected some more morphine into her IV. Not enough to put her under, just enough to take the edge off the pain.

To his chagrin he was called back to the emergency room. He spoke to her softly, but she didn't respond. He instructed a nurse to stay with her until he returned.

He closed his eyes for a moment when he heard a soft sob come from the narrow hospital bed.

Chapter 6

Mercy, Chels, you look like a pale little Madonna!"

Chelsea looked up at gorgeous George smiling down at her, Elliot at her side.

"Why aren't you in Boston?" Chelsea asked, frowning.

"I got in last night. It's now today, morning to be exact. Never again will you go jogging without me. Was that head of yours in medieval England?"

"No, in San Francisco, in 1854, but it wasn't my fault."

"We know," Elliot said, gently squeezing Chelsea's hand. "You look good, Chelsea, a lot better than you did after your surgery."

"You saw me then? I don't remember you, Elliot."

"Well, I didn't get to see the pretty stitches on your belly, but David assured me that they were the best he'd ever seen."

Chelsea closed her eyes a moment against Elliot's wicked grin and her own dire embarrassment at her encounter with *Dr.* Winter, not just David Winter.

Elliot felt George's elbow in his ribs and said, "When you're feeling better, remind me to tell you about the time George came out of the anesthetic singing the French national anthem."

"I didn't know you'd had any surgery, George," Chelsea said, momentarily diverted from her thoughts, just as Elliot had hoped she'd be.

"She did, and scared the wits out of me. I remember finding her clutching her stomach, huddled against the refrigerator."

"Wearing your bathrobe," George added.

"At least yours was legitimate, George. There can be nothing more lowering than to be hit by a stoned moped," Chelsea said.

"She's speaking Georgette Heyer," George said. "She must be feeling better."

"You might know that the fellow didn't have a single injury," Elliot said. "Does that make you feel better?"

"I'm going to put a contract out on him."

"On who?" David asked, coming into the room. "Not me, I hope."

Chelsea felt every bone in her body shudder with embarrassment. She couldn't bring herself to look at him.

Chelsea didn't say a word, and David, put out by her ridiculous attitude, said, "You could thank me, Chelsea. I didn't let them shave you."

She gasped, and Elliot said quickly, shooting a quelling glance toward David, "Well, Chelsea, George and I brought you some obscenely fattening chocolates. George thought flowers would be a waste. She said you'd prefer stuffing your face."

"What I would prefer," Chelsea said, tight-lipped, "is to stuff them in David's face."

"No gratitude in this life," David said with a mock sigh.

"You operated on me!" Chelsea struggled to sit up, felt a terrible tugging pain in her stomach and flopped back down. "I know the law, Dr. Winter. You can't operate on anyone unless they sign consent forms!"

"You did," David said.

"I wouldn't! I didn't!"

"Would you care to see them?"

"Now, Chels," George began.

But Chelsea was now remembering signing something. "You tricked me," she said, lowering her eyebrows and indulging him with her most menacing stare. "It was something about my will—"

"No, that's what you said. I explained that it was a consent to do a laparotomy."

"Lapawhatamy? What the dickens is that? You didn't explain that, David. I am going to sue your socks off. I'm going to—"

"Just a moment, Chelsea," David said. "You have some visitors who gave me all the permission in the world to do whatever I wanted to."

"Cookie!"

"Comment ça va, mon petit chou?"

"Dad! Mother!" Chelsea gasped. "You were in Paris, Mother, you were... oh, I'm fine and I am not a little cabbage!"

Mrs. Mimi Lattimer, a very pretty woman in her early fifties with hair as black as her daughter's, leaned over Chelsea and pecked her lightly on her cheek. "I just flew back from Paris last evening, *ma chère*. Then we get this call from Elliot. *Et voilà! Ton père* got us on the first flight to San Francisco this morning."

Dr. Harold Lattimer, tanned, fit and with his daughter's vivid blue eyes, kissed her other cheek. "We'll be hearing fractured French for a while, Chels. You were plotting in the middle of the street, weren't you?"

"No, Daddy, really." She interrupted herself, saying abruptly, "Daddy, this *man* operated on me without telling me! I want you to smack him, sue him, send him back to Boston!"

"Now, Cookie," Dr. Lattimer said, "this man took very good care of you. He told me all about your injury and what was done. I approve. You were a bit of a pain in the butt, weren't you, in the emergency room? Caused a bit of commotion?"

Chelsea stared at her father. "There is no more loyalty toward offspring in this world," she said.

Dr. Lattimer laughed, revealing teeth as straight and white as his daughter's. "Cookie, don't be an idiot. Tell you what, all these folk are going to be getting you up soon. How about if I walk you around?"

Chelsea moaned, wrapping her arms about herself. "I don't want to move, not even for you, Daddy."

David, who had been watching this interplay, began to frown. He looked sharply at Elliot, and Elliot, understanding that look, just grinned and shrugged. If he was seeing an example of parents not caring about their only child, David thought, he would jump off the Golden Gate.

"Elliot," he said, his voice sharp, "I want to speak to you."

Saved by the dentist, Elliot thought, for before he could respond Dr. Lattimer said, "Tell us, Dr. Winter, when is this girl going to be released into her parents' custody?"

"Another three days. We'll want to build her strength back up before she goes home. Are you and Mrs. Lattimer staying?"

"Bien sûr!" said Mimi Lattimer, beaming at this very acceptable man. "Our little *chou* needs tender loving care." She paused a moment, her busy fingers twisting the beautiful pearls around her neck. "I wonder how the dear French would say that."

Chelsea moaned. Any port in a storm became a madhouse when her parents arrived. She didn't open her eyes when she felt David take her wrist. His fingers were long, she knew, the nails blunt.

"Why don't you go talk to your lawyer?" she asked when he released her hand.

He laughed softly, and without thinking, without realizing her parents were standing on one side of the bed, George and Elliot on the other, he gently rubbed his knuckles over her cheek. "Keep thinking nasty thoughts. It'll take your mind off your belly."

Harold Lattimer shot an interested look toward his wife.

"L'amour," Mimi announced.

David straightened like a shot. To Elliot's amusement a dull flush spread over his face.

Chelsea, who hadn't caught what her mother had said, muttered, "Daddy, would you please remove this lecherous maniac? I will decide what to do and tell you later."

"L'amour sans..." Mimi searched frantically, shrugged, smiled charmingly and added, *"Sans le or la recognition."*

Chelsea stared up at her mother. "Mother, have you slipped a cog? Do you have jet lag?"

"Why do you call this nice man a lecher, Cookie?" Mimi asked. "A maniac I can understand, but a lecher?"

George said, "Chelsea is very modest, Mimi. As I well know, in the emergency room nothing is sacred."

"You're right, of course, George," Mimi said. "That wouldn't be at all romantic, now would it?"

"Mother!" Chelsea wailed.

David said firmly, "I think it's time for Chelsea to rest a bit. Why don't you all come back this afternoon?"

"George and I will drop you off at the Fairmont," Elliot said to Dr. and Mrs. Lattimer. "That's where you're staying, right?"

"Always, dear boy," Mimi said. "When Chelsea visits us there, her plotting brain goes haywire. It's that grand, ornate lobby, you know, all that—"

"Mother!"

"Oui, oui, ma chère." Mimi patted her daughter's cheek. "You do what Dr. Winter tells you, all right? Your papa and I will come back later. And don't excite yourself."

Harold Lattimer said thoughtfully, "I believe that in French it would translate much differently, my love."

"Daddy!"

There was dead silence in the room. David couldn't think of a thing to say, and Chelsea looked as though she were ready to spit nails.

"All right, Cookie, we're off now. Do as you're told, all right?"

"Ha!"

The door closed behind the Lattimers and the Mallorys. David shook himself. "All right, Chelsea, time for you to walk at least to the bathroom."

She did have to go, Chelsea thought, and a bedpan was the most humiliating idea imaginable. She tried to sit up, felt a tugging pain and gasped. "My stitches!"

"It's okay. Let me help you." David eased her upright, then swung her legs over the side of the bed.

"I don't think this is such a good idea."

"Yes, it is," he said firmly. "Come on now."

Chelsea became aware that her nightgown was open in the back and muttered, "This is disgusting."

David, whose attention was entirely on helping her negotiate her way across the room, didn't respond. She was bent over like a very old person, and the top of her head came to his shoulder. He tightened his arm around her. "You're doing great, Chelsea. Can you manage in the bathroom by yourself?"

Chelsea drew a deep breath, turned to face him and said in the meanest voice she could manufacture. "If you think you're going to hold my hand in there you're not only a lecher, you're weird!"

"I wish," David said, now thoroughly irritated, "that you would stop behaving like an idiot. I am a doctor, *your* doctor, and you're a patient. Can't you get that through your silly head?"

Chelsea tried to pull away from him, felt a searing pain twist in her belly and gasped. She lowered her head, trying not to cry.

To David's combined chagrin and relief Dr. Dennis Madson opened the door at that moment. He stood quietly, his eyes widening at the sight of Dr. Winter holding his patient very closely in the open bathroom doorway.

"I'll be back in about five minutes," he said, and backed out of the room.

"Are you all right, Chelsea?" David asked.

She nodded. "I want to go to the bathroom."

He helped her inside the door, then closed it. He leaned against the wood for a moment, his eyes closed. What a bizarre mess, he thought, his jaw tightening. All that manufactured foolery Elliot had let slip was just that: foolery. From the short time he'd been with Chelsea's parents he could see—any idiot could see— that they were nuts, but loved her to distraction. And Chelsea loved them. Then what about poor Chelsea starving? He remembered his worry about her surviving on leftover salad from the Alta Mira and ground his teeth. He couldn't wait to get his hands on Elliot Mallory.

David eyed the bathroom door, aware that his entire body was tense with worry. Come on out, Chelsea. I want you back in bed where I can keep an eye on you. I don't want you falling in there.

The door opened just an instant before he was prepared to go in and bring her out.

"You okay?"

She nodded, not looking at him.

"Let's walk back to the bed." He didn't support her this time, merely walked beside her, his arms ready if she faltered.

He tucked her in, then straightened. "You're awfully quiet all of a sudden," he said.

"Yes," she said. "David, I've got a TV show in a week and a half, then a trip for a promotion back to New York. Will I be all right by then?"

TV? A promotion in New York? For sure she was starving!

"You should be." He couldn't help himself, and added, "Who's paying for all this?"

"My publishing house. Why?"

"I just wondered, that's all." He planned to kill Elliot Mallory. He glanced down at his watch. "Time for a pill and a nap. I'll see you later."

David quietly opened her door and peered in. He heard her say to George, "You should have seen Mother when she got back from Germany. I had to goose-step for her to get her to stop with her *danke*'s, darling."

"Hi, George, Chelsea," he said. "How do you feel?"

"Fine," Chelsea said. "I want out of here, David."

"In a couple of days," he said. "Not before."

"She's feeling much better," George said, smiling fondly at Chelsea. "She's already been arguing with me."

"She argued with me, screamed at me and said she was feeling like the proverbial something the cat dragged in. I don't think that's a particularly significant sign, George."

George smiled her dazzling, beautiful smile and rose. "I'll let you talk to your doctor a bit, love. I'll go to the third floor and bug Elliot."

"She is so exquisite," Chelsea said, sighing.

"Who? George? Yes, I suppose so."

Chelsea frowned at him, but he was looking at her chart. "You were polite to Dr. Madson, weren't you?" he asked, looking up.

"No, I threw my water bottle at him."

"Chels!"

"He didn't make me take my clothes off. Of course I was polite."

"He didn't have to," David said. "He already saw everything he needed to see. Besides, your clothes are already off."

Chelsea growled, then winced.

David very carefully moved any possible weapon and said, "Now be just as polite to me, if you please." He took her pulse, then placed the stethoscope against her heart. Chelsea found herself staring at his thick chestnut hair and the small curls at his nape. She quickly looked away, furious with herself.

"Sounds good," David said.

"You really do look silly in that white coat," Chelsea said.

"Would you trust me more as a doctor if I were wearing jeans and a sweatshirt?"

"No."

David drew a deep breath and said, "I need to change the bandage on your belly now. Are you going to cooperate?"

She just stared at him, color creeping over her cheeks.

"Chelsea, I'm not going to call the nurse until I have your assurance that you won't throw a fit."

She licked her lower lip. "I don't want you to," she said.

Irritated, he said, "Look, lady, I've already seen you in great detail. I assure you I won't be driven crazy with lust."

She looked at him, her lips a thin line.

"How can you have been raised by a father who's a doctor and be so ridiculous about this? You are a patient, utterly sexless, and that's it."

She was being silly; she knew it. "I'm sorry. Go ahead."

He stared at her suspiciously for a moment, then nodded. He called the nurse.

Chelsea lay rigidly, her eyes tightly closed, as David bared her stomach and gently peeled off the bandage. He spoke to the nurse, a very different voice from the one he used to her, she thought. She winced a bit, and he said, "Sorry about that, Chelsea. Just a moment longer. You look great."

Yeah, I just bet I do, she thought. She felt lousy, her head ached and she didn't think her stomach would ever feel normal again.

She heard David giving instructions to the nurse. "Now," he said, after he'd pulled her nightgown back down, "I don't think you need that IV any longer." He gently pulled the needle out of the vein in her arm and rubbed her skin.

"Ah," he said straightening, "here are your parents. I'll see you later, Chelsea."

"Much later," Chelsea said, but very softly.

"Ma chère!"

While her mother enthusiastically embraced her, Chelsea saw her dad speaking to David. Her dad nodded, smiled and shook David's hand. Ratty men, she thought. They stick together like a herd, or a gaggle, or a crash, or... a murder of ravens. Could that possibly be right? It sounded awfully silly.

David heard Dr. Lattimer say in a loud stage whisper to Chelsea, "Obvious hero material, Cookie."

He quickly eased out of the room. He didn't want to hear what Chelsea would say to that.

You miss her, you stupid bastard. David sighed, dropped to the floor of his living room and did twenty-five fast push-ups.

He checked the clock, set up his VCR and inserted a tape. He turned on a talk show, a local San Francisco show, and some ten minutes later Chelsea came on. He stared. He hadn't seen her for nearly a week now. The couple of times he'd called, she'd told him she was busy. It was George who had told him when Chelsea would be on TV.

She was wearing a dark blue silk dress, very nearly the color of her sparkling eyes, very high heels and a big, infectious grin.

She looked sleek, very sophisticated and very beautiful.

Poor starving Chelsea, indeed.

He sat back, at first nervous for her. He shouldn't have bothered, he thought some five minutes later. She was very articulate, fielding impertinent questions with marvelous aplomb. She oozed self-confidence. And, of course, the host and hostess talked about her success.

When the show was over David wandered out onto his deck and stared toward the Bay. Elliot had definitely done a number on him. But why? He had a chilling thought. If they had distorted things about

Chelsea, what had they told her about him? He intended to find out—now.

He grabbed his jacket, roared Nancy into life and sped toward the Mallorys' house in Pacific Heights.

Chapter 7

David pulled into the Mallorys' driveway, grimly relieved to see Elliot's Jaguar beside George's infamous Porsche, Esmerelda. He bounded out of the car and strode to the front door.

He didn't bother with the doorbell, just pounded the wood with his fist. He heard a distant "Just a minute!"

George opened the door. "David!"

He didn't pause, didn't at first notice that George, beautiful George, looked like a frazzled wreck. "Where's Elliot?"

"I'll get him," she said, eyeing him a moment. She waved toward the living room. "Have a seat, David."

He was pacing about when Elliot said from the doorway. "What's up, David?"

George, on his heels, said sharply, "Did you hear from Chelsea? Is she all right?"

"Of course she's all right. I just saw her charming self on TV. That isn't what I wanted. Damn it, you two, why the hell did you tell me that Chelsea was a poor, starving little waif, ignored by her parents? And it *was* 'tell.' At least, you did more than intimate. Well?"

George jerked about at the piercing sound of Alex screaming.

"Anna is away with her sick sister," Elliot said, rubbing his forehead with a tired hand. "You stay here, love, and try to calm this infant down and I'll see to the other infant upstairs."

"What did you say you wanted, David?" George asked, obviously distracted by the rising cries.

David saw the weariness on her face and drew up short, feeling guilt mix with his righteous ire.

"Alex is colicky," George said. She swiped her hair away from her face, searched her hair for a bobby pin and, not finding one, looked as if she'd burst into tears. "Oh, rats," she said. "Everything comes in threes. This should all be amusing, I suppose. Now you've come to rant, so get on with it."

"I'm sorry," David said. "This will just take a minute, and then I'll be out of your hair." Poor reference, he thought, but for the moment he held his ground.

"What?"

"Why did you guys lie to me about Chelsea?"

George glared at him.

"Well?"

She turned when Elliot trotted down the stairs, Alex in his arms. The baby was red faced from yelling. Now he was hiccuping, his head on his father's shoulder,

Elliot's large hand moving in gentle circles over his back.

"What's up?" Elliot asked.

"This man," George said to her husband as she waved a hand toward David, "is accusing us of lying to him about Chelsea."

Elliot cocked a black brow. "Yeah? So?"

Alex gave a particularly loud hiccup.

George, tired, at the end of her tether, snapped, "I'll tell you why, you ridiculous eastern idiot! You're so confounded uptight, unreasonable and just plain stupid . . . you don't deserve anybody as lively and intelligent and successful as Chelsea! Oh, yes, she earns rings around you, Doctor! I thought maybe you two would be good for each other, but obviously I was wrong! She doesn't deserve a man as opposite as you are!"

David was suddenly squirming. He'd never before heard George raise her voice, much less rake anyone down as she'd just done him. "Oh, hell, look, George, Elliot, I didn't mean—"

"I know," Elliot said. "We did do a number on both you and Chelsea. I guess people shouldn't try to matchmake." He added ruefully, "You two are so bloody different. George is right. Forgive us for interfering. It would never work between you, in any case."

"What did you tell Chelsea about me?"

George gave him a nasty look. "I told her you'd been impotent with your wife, and that she had laughed at you, and that's why you turned weird on her that night and insulted her about never being serious."

David was momentarily speechless. "You *what*?"

Elliot handed Alex to his mother. "Let me show you out, David," he said. "I think that about covers it. Excuse us now."

"Oh, no," David muttered. "George didn't. She wouldn't!" He looked hopefully at Elliot, praying George had made up that awful bit of horror.

"She did," Elliot said, trying to control the grin that was fighting to appear. "What I found amazing was the fact that Chelsea would buy such a story. After all, what man would go around telling people how he couldn't perform and his wife had laughed at him? But Chelsea didn't question it. She just wanted to take care of you, get you over your hurt and all that. Now, David, why don't you go away? Both George and I are ready to drop. I swear to you that we'll leave you alone—you and your love life, that is—from now on."

David left and drove around for an hour. He ran out of gas near St. Francis Wood. He looked stupidly at his gas gauge, then began to laugh.

Chelsea loved New York. Her publishing house had not only paid for her appearance at the yearly conference, but also, in a spate of good will, offered her a limo to the airport. To all her business meals she wore her favorite gray fedora and her gray alpaca cloak. They made her feel confident and jaunty, sharpened her step, in short, made her feel like the neatest thing to hit the city. She saw old friends, made new ones, was feted until she was ready to drop. Writing was a lonely business, just you and your computer. That was why, she knew, that writers, when they were released into the world, danced and laughed and talked until they were dizzy. And it felt so good to hear the people who came to the autograph session tell her how much they enjoyed her novels.

But she tired so easily and quickly. The wretched surgery, she thought, angry at her body's betrayal.

She dropped into bed each night feeling like a wrung-out sponge. Then she thought of David and squirmed with embarrassment.

You lecher, go away and leave me alone! But he didn't, and despite her attempts to control her wayward memories, she found herself playing and replaying their last meeting.

"Ah," he'd said, grinning as he came into her hospital room, "you're wearing lipstick. Ready to rejoin the world? I told you, didn't I, that I really like that peachy shade? Looks good with your flushed face."

"Shouldn't you be somewhere saving lives and stomping out disease?" she'd asked in a bitchy voice.

The jerk had the gall to grin at her. "Bear your belly for me and I'll start stomping."

"You are incredibly thick-skinned," Chelsea had said, wishing she could smack that grin off his face. "Doesn't anything get through to you?"

"And you look incredibly sexy," David responded, seemingly oblivious of her snit.

She sucked in her breath. "You're a doctor and I'm a sexless patient. Remember your sermon, Dr. Winter?"

"As of this afternoon you're no longer a sexless patient, Chelsea. Your parents are at this very moment downstairs clearing away all the details with administration. You'll shortly be a free woman."

She said nothing, and he added, his voice suddenly very serious, "Your folks are going to stay with you for a couple of days, aren't they?"

"Yes, I couldn't get rid of them even if I threatened to move back in with them."

David felt immense relief to hear that. "Good," he said. "Get as much exercise as you can, but don't go overboard. And force yourself to straighten up. The stitches won't pull out. One last thing, Chelsea, come in next Tuesday to get the stitches out."

"Who's going to have the pleasure of doing the snipping?"

"You want me to?" he asked, moving closer and taking her unwilling hand.

She tried to jerk it away, but he wouldn't let her go. "No! As a matter of fact, if I never again see the backs of your ears I'll be eternally grateful!"

"All this drama because I took care of you?" His voice was teasing, and she readily jumped to the bait.

"You treated me like a slab of meat, you lecher, and you *looked* at me!"

"Yes, all of you, as a matter of fact. Very nice."

She growled and hissed, and he continued to smile. She remembered all too clearly that he'd examined every inch of her. It was too much. She closed her eyes tightly, willing away that very clear image.

"But you know," he continued thoughtfully after a moment, "as I recall, you do have a major flaw—a corn on the second toe of your left foot."

Her eyes flew open. "Get out!" She managed this time to jerk her hand out of his grasp.

"You know something, Chelsea?" he said in a mild, nearly disinterested voice. "You irritate me more than any woman I've ever known. You are silly and ignorant, and I hope to heaven that the next time you get smacked by a moped it will be near another hospital. Oh, yeah, you write trash."

She threw her water carafe at him.

"Be certain not to get your bandage wet," he said, retrieving the carafe and tossing it onto the bed. He watched the remaining water soak through the sheet.

He gave her a mock salute and left.

"Obnoxious jerk!" she yelled after him.

"Oh, damn and blast!" Chelsea said now into the darkness of her hotel room. Wretched, miserable man! I will not think of you anymore, except to congratulate myself on never having to see you again.

David buried himself at the hospital, and Elsa, eyeing him with renewed hope, tried to make herself indispensable. But he wouldn't bite. Nothing. There was still a lot of gossip going around about that Lattimer woman and the scene she'd caused. And Dr. Winter's reaction. And the way he'd haunted her hospital room until she'd left. Even now, Elsa heard him being teased by administrators and other doctors.

David found himself one late afternoon near a bookstore and wandered in. He didn't mean to, but he found himself studying titles and books in the romance section. Sure enough, they had four different books of Chelsea's. He winced at the outrageous covers and the ridiculous come-on write-ups on the back. Surely she couldn't have anything to do with all that nonsense. Of course she didn't. He remembered her moaning and telling him that the covers were getting more and more dreadful—not at all romantic, just more and more skin, and fake rapturous looks—and the write-ups, "Argh!" He smiled as he read the back of one of her novels. *He was hot-blooded, handsome—and American. And now she was his property, bought and paid for.*

He shook his head, but picked up all four titles, presenting them with great panache to the clerk at the counter. To his utter astonishment he found that he couldn't put the first novel down. He was thrown into Victorian England in the early 1850s, and he could practically taste the food they were eating, almost picture the carriages and the clothing and feel the London fog. The characters were real, complex and sympathetic, and he couldn't wait to turn the next page.

He read until three o'clock in the morning. He set the book on his nightstand, lay back in bed and thought about it. He'd enjoyed the hell out of the story, laughed at the continuous, very amusing repartee between the hero—that hot-blooded American— and the heroine. He found himself wondering about the sex scenes. Her hot-blooded hero was also an excellent lover. And a marvelous mixture of Chelsea's Mark I and Mark II heroes. It was odd, he reflected, on the edge of sleep, to read about sex from a woman's perspective. It was honest, but, of course, the heroine adored sex with the hero. What if she hadn't? What if the hot-blooded hero had botched the entire affair?

Not in a novel. Especially not in a romantic novel. What had Chelsea said once? Oh, yes, she wrote escapist literature, fantasy to a certain extent, because what woman would want to escape to a beer-gutted hero who was clumsy and selfish? That, he thought, smacked of disappointment.

He found himself wondering about her sexual experience. She certainly seemed to know what she was talking about. Had she had many lovers? For all he knew her very intricate love scenes could have been taken from her own experiences with men.

He shook his head in the dark. That didn't make sense. He remembered all too clearly her unbelievable reaction to him in the emergency room. He pictured her slender, very white body in his mind, and felt his body respond instantly. She did, he now knew from firsthand experience, have a very nice bottom.

Damn her silly eyes, he wanted to see her again. He closed his eyes in excruciating embarrassment. He still couldn't believe George had told Chelsea he'd been impotent.

The days passed quickly as David immersed himself in one crisis after another. He decided finally, his misery having reached its saturation point, that if she wanted a Mark I hero, like her hot-blooded American, she'd get it. With a dash of Mark II thrown in for good measure.

Chelsea kicked off her shoes and plopped down on her sofa. She was exhausted, but also exhilarated. She'd had a ball in New York, accomplished a good deal of business, and even had lunch with the chairman of the board of her publishing house, a charming man, handsome and very articulate. Now, she thought, she had to get to work. Her mind had obligingly plotted during every free moment she'd had—when David hadn't intruded—and now her fingers were itching to get to the keyboard.

If only she weren't so blasted tired. Her eyes closed, and she drifted off.

She was awakened by the doorbell. She cocked a half-closed eye toward the obnoxious sound, forcing herself to rise. It was a delivery boy carrying a box of flowers.

"What?"

"Miss Lattimer?"

"Yes, but—"

"For you, ma'am."

And he was gone before she could even try to tip him. She stood barefoot in her entryway staring down at the box. No one had ever before sent her flowers. She opened the box slowly and gasped at the two dozen long-stemmed red roses.

She knew who had sent them, but nonetheless she very quickly opened the card. She read, "Welcome home, Chelsea. I'll pick you up at seven o'clock Friday night. Wear something long and sexy." And it was signed simply, "David."

"I wouldn't go to a wake with you," she said aloud, but she very carefully arranged the beautiful roses in her one vase and set it on her coffee table.

It was all very unexpected, she thought a while later as she slowly drank a glass of white wine. She clearly remembered his saying that she irritated him more than any woman he had ever known. Then why did he want to see her again? Something long and sexy, huh?

She was dozing on her sofa, half her attention on the TV, when it suddenly occurred to her. The realization, in fact, hit her squarely between the eyes. *No man would admit to having failed in bed. No man, even if he'd had a problem, would admit to having his wife laugh at him.*

George! Oh, no!

"I've got to be the most gullible, silly woman alive!" she nearly shouted to her empty living room. "Just you wait, George Mallory!"

It was close to nine o'clock in the evening when she pulled into the Mallorys' driveway. Thank God both their cars were there.

She slammed the car door loudly and marched to the front door. She lifted her hand to press the doorbell.

Was that a giggle she heard?

She frowned and pressed the buzzer.

Was that a curse? From Elliot?

She heard a "Just a moment," spoken in an oddly breathless voice, and the sound of pattering bare feet. The door opened, reluctantly.

"Chelsea!"

She looked at George, breathtakingly beautiful and disheveled in one of Elliot's shirts, and gulped. Her hair was tousled, and her mouth looked a bit swollen, as if she'd been kissed a good dozen times with great enthusiasm.

"I, ah..." Deep, embarrassed gulp. "Did I come at a bad time, George?"

"Get rid of whoever it is!" she heard Elliot call from the living room. Then a nasty laugh, and another shout. "I know it's Chelsea. Be rude! Send her to David. Let the two of them fight it out."

George laughed at Chelsea's expression. "I would suggest that you call first before you come over, Chels, unless, that is, you want to see my gorgeous husband in the buff on the living room rug."

"But...oh, damn! I wanted to talk to you about David. George, he couldn't ever have *talked about* what he, well, couldn't do in bed. It's ridiculous. No man would—"

"True, and David's already attacked us. Now, my dear friend, call me tomorrow. Goodbye."

"Go see David, Chelsea," Elliot called from the living room. "I imagine that he's dying to see you!"

"This is awful," Chelsea said. "I'm sorry, George." And she fled.

The following evening, Friday, Chelsea stared at the clock, then down at her ratty blue jeans and frumpy sweatshirt. My rendition of long and sexy, she thought. She should have left, but somehow she hadn't been able to make herself do so.

The doorbell rang promptly at seven.

"Go away!" she shouted through the door.

"Open the door, Chelsea, or I'll kick it in."

David was saying that? What the devil was going on, anyway?

She opened the door. "Hi," she said in a very inadequate voice. He'd gotten her again, she thought, her eyes roving over his body. He was wearing jeans as old as hers and a flannel shirt that had seen better days a decade ago.

"Hello, yourself," David said, grinning down at her. He stepped inside, grabbed her before she could move and swept her up against him. He kissed her very thoroughly.

Chelsea was too startled to react. When he finally eased the pressure on her mouth she gasped out, "You idiot! Put me down! You shouldn't be here! What are you doing?"

David gave her another tight squeeze, then set her away from him. He was beaming. "I read several of your books. Right now I'm your hot-blooded American who swept into the heroine's life and knocked her socks off."

"You're an idiot!"

"You're repeating your insults," he said. At her continued outraged expression, David managed a wounded look. "But, Chels, isn't that what your heroines like? To find a man who's as strong as they are, who will give them both heaven and hell? Who will master them despite what they think they want?"

"This is real life, David Winter!"

"Aha, so you agree that your novels are sheer nonsense."

Chelsea slammed her fist into his stomach.

He obligingly grunted and continued smiling down at her.

"You are the most ignorant, stupid, ridiculous man—"

"I like what you're wearing. It isn't particularly the kind of long I had in mind, but that sweatshirt's sexy, as well, something out of my mother's attic."

She frowned at him, turned on her bare heel and marched into the living room. He followed her, smiling at the rigid set of her shoulders and the very nice swing of her bottom. She turned abruptly and said, "I shouldn't have hit you. A writer is much too articulate to resort to violence. Now—"

"Can I have a glass of wine before you do me in?"

Chelsea disappeared into the kitchen, returning a few minutes later with two glasses of wine. "Here," she said, thrusting one at him.

"Thank you, you're a marvelous hostess, all warm and caring and—"

"Can it, David. Now what I was saying before you rudely interrupted me is that if you have indeed read some of my novels, the heroines are closer to eighteen than to twenty-eight, and virgins. I simply arrange circumstances so that they meet the *right* man for them. I might add, Dr. Winter, that men today are incompetent jerks, arrogant, still chauvinistic—"

"You've never been to bed with me, Chelsea. How do you know I'm incompetent?"

He spoke mildly, looking at her with a modicum of interest. She wanted to growl at him, but stopped herself.

Get a hold of yourself, idiot! He's just trying to pile you, make you say ridiculous things and lose your temper.

"Thank you for the roses," she said, tilting up her chin. "They're beautiful."

"Thank you. My pleasure."

"As I said, David," she continued calmly, but with a definite glint in her eyes, "I am twenty-eight years old. I have a lot of women friends. Some of those who are married find themselves resorting to technology—"

"Technology? What does that mean?"

"I refuse to get more specific!" She flushed, wanted to kick herself, but forced herself onward. "Now those who aren't married, tell me that the guys they meet all want to hop in the sack. That's all, nothing more. And that is why my heroes are tender, talented—"

"Tasteful? Torpid? Torpedoes?"

Chelsea closed her eyes a moment. "I'm going to belt you again if you don't shut up!"

"All right," he said agreeably, but she heard the amusement in his voice. "Now tell me, what is your experience?"

"Another thing," she continued, ignoring him and speaking in the most evil voice she could manage. "You men all get your jollies—reaffirm your macho virility and all that nonsense—through violent movies and your stupid Westerns!"

"You've got a point," he said.

Chelsea blinked at him, totally taken aback. "What game are you playing now, David?"

He shrugged and sat down on her sofa. "No game. Now what is your experience with men?"

She stood in front of him, her hands on her hips. Well, one hand on her hip; the other was holding the remnants of her wine. She set down the glass with a thwap.

"You've never been married, have you, Chelsea?"

"No, I haven't, and I don't think I ever will. As for my experience, Doctor, let us say that I, too, very much enjoy reading about a hero who can not only enjoy himself but also the heroine, and vice versa. It's a marvelous fantasy," she added, trying for sarcasm.

David looked at her for a long, thoughtful moment. "I see," he said finally. "Have you ever been in love, Chelsea? Ever wanted a man?"

"No! And tell me, Doctor, what does *want* mean in your marvelous lexicon?"

"As in desire, lust after, sigh over, make cute little noises, yell when—"

"Stop it! The answer is no, and frankly, as Rhett would say, 'I don't give a damn.'"

"Do you plan to spend your life experiencing pleasure vicariously? Through made-up characters?"

That drew her up short. Dear heavens, she thought blankly, is that what I'm doing? "That smacks of voyeurism," she said aloud, her voice thin and high.

He grinned at her. "I've got a wager for you, Chelsea."

"The Friday night poker game isn't until next week," she said.

"Not that kind of wager. Do you want to hear it?"

"I think I'll get another glass of wine first," she said, and left the living room.

He said very softly, "The Mark I hero has become cunning. You'd best make it a very large glass of wine, sweetheart."

Chapter 8

Well, what is this wager of yours?"

"Drink a bit more of that wine and I'll tell you."

She did, set the glass on the coffee table and sank to the floor, tucking her bare feet under her. "Well?"

"You seem to have had crummy experiences with men," David said matter-of-factly.

"No, not crummy, probably just the same kind of experiences that many women have had, I guess."

"Ah, yes, the proverbial wham, bam, rolling over and deep snores."

"Don't be crude." She dropped her eyes a moment, knowing that she wasn't being honest. Two men did not a statistical analysis make. And they'd been young and inexperienced, just as she had been. She sighed. At the tender ages of twenty-one and twenty-four she'd been willing and eager to fall in love. Indeed, she'd believed for a while that she had been in love. But now she knew she hadn't.

"Your wager, David?"

"I want to make love to and with you."

She stared at him. This, she thought blankly, from a stuffed shirt, uptight doctor from Boston who'd once accused her of not being serious enough?

"Why?" she blurted out.

"Damned if I know," he said thoughtfully, but she saw that gleam of amusement in his eyes.

"Does this go along with being a doctor and wanting to save lives and stomp out disease? As in, see this poor confused woman who needs a man?"

"I don't think being a doctor necessarily equates to being a good lover. But if it pleases you to think so—"

"It doesn't, and this is ridiculous!"

"I've always thought that every woman needed a good man."

"And you're applying?"

"For part of it, anyway. The wager is this, Chelsea. Make love with me. If you don't like it, I'll order every male resident at the hospital to read every one of your books. Look at it this way," he continued quickly, seeing that she was probably on the brink of colorfully describing his antecedents, "even if you found the experience a total and complete bore, you'd probably save a good half-dozen guys from continuing in their doubtless selfish and egocentric ways with women. I doubt that any of them, myself included, have ever read about sex from a woman's perspective. An eye-opener, I promise you."

She thought about some of her love scenes, spun from an ideal model, so to speak. She looked at him thoughtfully. He was a beautiful man, no doubt about that. His jaw, she noticed for the first time, was as stubborn as hers. And she did like him when she wasn't furious with him. She probably liked him a lot more than he deserved. And he'd already seen her in the buff, so she wouldn't have to be too embarrassed.

"I don't know," she said finally, fiddling with her wineglass.

David, who had expected to be castigated to the fullest utility of her powers of speech, felt a jolt of very intense desire. "You could," David said, trying to sound like a detached scientist, "consider it an experiment, I suppose." He shrugged. "Who knows? The sky might fall. The earth might move. You might like it."

"Are you talking about tonight?"

He gave her a wicked smile. "What better time than the present? I have this awful feeling that even if you agreed to our wager now, you would chicken out by tomorrow."

That was a definite maybe! She shifted her weight, stretching her legs out in front of her, leaning back and balancing herself on her hands. She eyed him again, very searchingly. "Why do you want to make love to me? I seem to remember that I'm the most irritating woman you've ever met. And don't you dare say 'damned if you know' again!"

"Okay, I won't." And he said nothing more.

"Well? Why?"

"I find myself thinking at very odd moments that you're incredibly adorable. Like your heroes, I want to take you and love you until you yell with pleasure."

"A nice fantasy," she said.

"We'll see."

"I haven't agreed yet," she said sharply.

"What about George and Elliot? Do you think George resorts to technology and Elliot rolls over and snores like a pig?"

"Of course not. They're . . . different."

"I don't consider either of us particularly run-of-the-mill."

Chelsea fell silent, her mind skipping from one objection to another. He was also, she decided, a very good talker. She said in a rush, "What if I like it, and you?"

"Ah," David said, leaning forward, his hands clasped between his knees. "Then I would imagine we would be constrained to continue the experiment, to verify and recheck, of course." What the hell was he getting himself into? he wondered. What if she agreed and it was a fiasco? He came out of his fog at the sound of her voice. "What did you say? I'm sorry."

"I said yes."

Now, David thought frantically, what would a Mark I hero do? Grab her and carry her into the bedroom? Show triumph with a demonic laugh? Think about submission and surrender? He grinned at his thoughts, rose and stretched. No, he thought, he'd just have to be himself and hope it was good enough. After all, he was a *good* man, wasn't he?

"Well?" Chelsea asked, her eyes staring at his sneakered feet and moving upward. His thighs were thick, she saw, doubtless from jogging and swimming. She wondered if . . .

"Well, what?"

"The wager, David!"

"Actually, the wager is quite one-sided at the moment. What will you give me if I—we—turn out to be the greatest thing since sliced bread?"

"I will die of shock."

"That's a start, I guess," he said. "Come here, Chelsea. I want to make love with you in the bedroom. Your carpet doesn't look too thick and soft."

Chelsea gulped and slowly got to her feet. Standing in her bare feet, she didn't even come to his chin. "Oh, dear," she said, then stopped as he gently pulled her against him.

"A nice fit," he said, breathing in the sweet scent of her hair. He rubbed his large hands very lightly up and down her back, forcing himself to stay away from her bottom, for the moment at least. It occurred to him as he leaned down and gently began to nuzzle her ear that he had changed. Changed profoundly. This small, very mouthy woman made him laugh, made him see life from a slightly skewed angle, or maybe, he added silently, he'd lived most of his life according to rules that no longer fit him. It was certain that all signs of his incipient ulcer had disappeared. He wondered how that could be possible when she also made him want to wring her neck. And love her until they were both too weary even to snipe at each other.

He felt her stand on her tiptoes, and he sucked in his breath. Her breasts slid up his chest, and her belly was pressed firmly against him. Very slowly he brought his right hand around and cupped her chin. For someone who hadn't slept with a woman in a good many months, he was pleased at his restraint. Very lightly he kissed her pursed lips, not demanding, not forcing her in any way.

"You taste like shrimp salad," he said between nibbles on her throat.

"Sarah's shrimp salad is yummy. I'm not sure about this," Chelsea added in a very worried voice.

"Just relax. Isn't that what your heroes tell their heroines? Trust me? Give yourself to me?"

"Yes, sometimes, but—"

"But nothing. Stop worrying and kiss me again."

She did, with more enthusiasm this time. He tasted very good himself, she thought, and she liked what his hands were doing on her back. She pressed closer, sliding her arms over his shoulders. She was feeling warm, and very interested.

He slipped his hands beneath her sweatshirt, and she stiffened. Stop being an idiot, she told herself. You are not one of your heroines, nor are you a coy eighteen-year-old. You are also letting him control everything just as if you were a silly, helpless twit.

"You feel good, David," she said against his mouth. "Your body feels nice." To her immense delight she felt his entire body shudder with reaction. She also felt him hard and pressing against her stomach. She blinked. That felt very nice, too. It would stop, she thought, when he got down to basics.

"I'm not wearing a white coat now, Chelsea," he said, smiling down at her.

"No," she said. "No, you're not."

To her surprise he lifted her into his arms. She felt so good, David thought. When she nestled her face against his throat he began to believe that this was one of his finest ideas.

Her bed wasn't made, and David smiled, his gaze falling on a wispy pair of bikini panties tossed onto a chair. He guessed that this had been one of Sarah's days off.

He deposited her on the bed, then sat down beside her. He didn't touch her, simply smiled down at her.

She looked expectant, a bit wary, but her eyes gleamed.

"When I first met you at the Mallorys'," he said, taking her hand in his, "I thought, now there is a very cute woman. I've since changed my mind. You are intelligent, warm, unpredictable and very sexy. I like your hair. It's irrepressible, like you." He tangled his fingers into the black curls over her left ear.

Think of something witty to say, idiot, she told herself, but she couldn't. She moved her head so that her cheek was against his open palm.

"I always wanted to be blond, like George. Most of my heroines have light hair," she said.

"Oh, no," David said. "Don't you realize how enticing you are? The black hair and the very white skin?"

He moved his palm against her cheek, smiling. "I'd like to see more of that beautiful white skin, Chelsea." Before she could even think of objecting, he grasped her sweatshirt and pulled it over her head.

Chelsea felt dreadfully exposed, and her hands flew to cover her breasts.

"No, don't," David said, gently drawing her hands away. She found herself watching him as he looked at her. He looked very intent, and she realized that she wanted him to touch her. She squirmed just a bit.

David very lightly laid his open hand over her breast. He closed his eyes a moment, savoring the incredible softness and the tautening of her nipple. He could feel her heartbeat speed up. "Very beautiful," he said. "Very white." He began to trace the tip of his finger around each breast.

Chelsea was taken by surprise at her own reaction. She arched her back upward, wanting him to fondle her. Instead his hand roved downward to her jeans. "I don't like one course at a time," he explained, seeing that she might protest. "I like to see everything at once. Hold still, Chelsea."

He pulled her jeans down, her panties with them. He looked up the length of her body. Her legs were as white as the rest of her, long and straight, and sleekly muscled from jogging. He realized that his own heart was pounding.

"What are you looking at?" Chelsea asked, feeling nervous, embarrassed and exhilarated all at the same time. "You've already looked at every inch of me."

"It wasn't the same thing," David said. He traced the small scar on her belly. "Any more pain?"

"No, just an occasional pulling feeling."

"That will continue for a couple months more. Dr. Madson did an excellent job."

Chelsea didn't care a bit about Dr. Madson. She realized that she was lying naked, and David, the wretched man, was fully dressed. Very unfair, she thought.

"No, don't move, let me enjoy you just a bit more, Chelsea," he said, his eyes caressing her face.

"As I said, you've already seen me," Chelsea said, her voice sharp and breathless.

"Understand, Chelsea," he said, his eyes on the small triangle of black curls, "that when I first saw you in the emergency room I was scared out of my mind. I was completely in my doctor mode until I was certain you weren't dying. Then my reaction was very natural. I did look at you—in a subliminal sort of way, of course. You're very beautiful, you know." He lightly pressed his palm over her, his fingers searching, and Chelsea lurched up, gasping.

She said rather wildly, "I refuse to lie here any longer being examined. I would like to see you, and there's nothing at all subliminal about it!"

He grinned at her and rose. Never before had a man stripped for *her*. Her heroes did for her heroines, of course, but that wasn't anything like this, like real life. She loved it. He unbuttoned his shirt and shrugged out of it. "Very nice," she said, wanting to ape him, but she couldn't quite bring it off. His chest was muscular, but not muscle-bound, and she couldn't wait to sift her fingers through the tufts of chestnut hair. She discovered that she was holding her breath when he unzipped his jeans and pulled them off. His shorts and sneakers quickly followed. Then he simply stood in front of her, beautifully naked. Chelsea gulped. "You look like one of my heroes," she said.

"Do I now?"

Her eyes moved lower, and she felt her face begin to warm and flush. He was large, thrusting outward.... She unconsciously licked her lower lip.

David couldn't stand it anymore. He moaned at that very sensuous gesture and moved down onto the bed beside her.

"Let's neck," he said, and pulled her against him.

"Do I have to be serious?"

"Not a bit, just moan to let me know what you're feeling."

"You're a good kisser," she managed after several minutes.

He muttered something, and she felt his large hand cup her bottom. "This has got to be heaven," he said.

"Close to it," Chelsea said, her own hand stroking down his back to knead his buttocks.

David was in bad shape, and he knew it. It had been a long time, and he wanted to enter her, but, he thought, grinning to himself, despite his own state he wasn't a selfish pig, and the thought of bringing Chelsea pleasure, watching her face while she experienced pleasure with him, was a heady feeling. A powerful feeling.

When his fingers found her, she was moist and delightfully soft. "Heaven, indeed," he whispered, pressing more closely against her.

Chelsea forgot the wager, forgot everything but him and his deft fingers. "It's been a very long time," she said.

"How long, sweetheart?" he asked, moving above her and looking down into her eyes. His fingers continued their gentle foraging.

"About four years. I think I've atrophied."

"Four years!" He simply couldn't imagine such a thing.

"Yes, I really thought that I wouldn't be able...ah, David, that feels so...please!"

Her hand closed over him, and he winced at her enthusiasm. It was probably just as well, for it gave him a bit more control.

He slipped his finger inside her and gasped at her incredible warmth. "No, not at all atrophied," he said. "Chels, hold still, all right?"

But she couldn't, and it surprised her. "David," she whispered, and felt his fingers deepen their pressure. She whimpered at the taut, convulsive feelings rampaging through her body. "I don't believe this!" Then she threw back her head and cried out.

David watched her face, watched her eyes blink with astonishment, then close, watched the arch of her throat as she threw her head back.

"That's it," he said, his voice harsh and raw in his own ears.

When he eased down Chelsea wanted nothing more than to experience him, all of him. She heard him moan, felt him thrust into her, very carefully and slowly, and clasped her arms about his back.

"Chelsea," David said, and that was his last word. It was her turn, and her pleasure to watch his face at the moment of his climax.

"You feel so good," she said when he was pressed full-length against her.

David concentrated on returning to life as he knew it. Damn. That had been unbelievable, but over with too quickly. She was so soft and small and yielding to him. He felt like shouting with pleasure, so he kissed her, deeply.

"If you dare to move," she said with great conviction, "I will never speak to you again."

He didn't. "The light," he said.

"Just don't move," Chelsea said, and reached out to switch off the lamp beside her bed. There was only the faint light coming from the living room.

"I'm too heavy for you, Chelsea. I don't want to hurt you."

"Move and I'll do something awful to you."

"Tell you what," he began, and before she could protest he brought her with him onto her side.

"I don't believe this," Chelsea said, and fell asleep, her face nestled against his chest, her leg wedged between his, her fingers splayed in his hair.

"I don't think I do, either," David said, feeling somewhat bewildered. He'd known that he would enjoy making love with her, but this overwhelming sense of well-being, of belonging, of warmth, shook him a bit. He fell asleep, too, his hand possessively on her bottom.

It was Chelsea who woke him during the night. She wanted him, and though she didn't understand it, she accepted it. "Hold still," she whispered into the darkness when he started to move over her. "I want to examine you."

He laughed, then moaned.

And when he rose over her, lifting her, and loved her with exquisite care, her protests died in her throat.

She could only stare into the darkness as the intense sensations swamped her, flinging her into a maelstrom of pleasure.

When Chelsea awoke the following morning she blinked at the sound of a rich baritone coming from the shower.

"Oh, dear," she observed to her empty bedroom, "I think I lost that damned wager of his."

She began to laugh.

Yes, become a Silhouette subscriber and the celebratio goes on forever.

To begin with, we'll send you:

- 4 new Silhouette Intimate Moments novels—FREE
- an elegant, purse-size manicure set—FREE
- and an exciting mystery bonus—FREE

And that's not all! Special extras— Three more reasons to celebrate.

4. **Money-Saving Home Delivery.** That's right! When you subscribe to Silhouette Intimate Moments, the excitement, romance and faraway adventures of these novels can be yours for previewing in the convenience of your own home. Here's how it works. Every month, we'll deliver four new books right to your door. If you decide to keep them, they'll be yours for only $2.25 each. That's 25¢ less per book than what you pay in stores. And there's **no charge for shipping and handling.**

5. **Free Monthly Newsletter.** It's the indispensable insider's look at our most popular writers and their up-coming novels. Now you can have a behind-the-scenes look at the fascinating world of Silhouette! It's an added bonus you'll look forward to every month!

6. **More Surprise Gifts.** Because our home subscribers are our most valued readers, we'll be sending you additional free gifts from time to time—as a token of our appreciation.

This beautiful manicure set will be a useful and elegant item to carry in your handbag. Its rich burgundy case is a perfect expression of your style and good taste. And it's yours free in this amazing Silhouette celebration!

SILHOUETTE INTIMATE MOMENTS®

FREE OFFER CARD

4 FREE BOOKS

ELEGANT MANICURE SET —FREE

FREE MYSTERY BONUS

PLACE YOUR BALLOON STICKER HERE!

FREE HOME DELIVERY

FREE FACT-FILLED NEWSLETTER

MORE SURPRISE GIFTS THROUGHOUT THE YEAR—FREE

Yes! Please send me four Silhouette Intimate Moments novels **FREE**, along with my manicure set and my free mystery gift as explained on the opposite page.

CBM057

NAME

(PLEASE PRINT)

ADDRESS _____ APT. _____

CITY _____ STATE _____

ZIP _____

Chapter 9

Chelsea looked up to see David standing in the bathroom doorway, one of her towels knotted low around his hips.

"Hi," she said, her laughter dying in her throat. What would one of her heroines do if the marauder came into the bedroom after a night of pleasure wearing only a lavender towel?

"I have good news for you, Chelsea," he said, coming toward the bed.

"What?" she asked, burrowing down under the covers.

"You don't have to worry about atrophy, not anymore, at least."

He laughed deeply, a laugh rich with satisfaction.

She threw a pillow at him.

"Weak, Chels, very weak. Didn't you tell me that you never resorted to physical violence? That you always used wit to carry you through?"

He picked up the pillow and strode to the bed. "I like the covers-to-the-chin bit," he said.

"I hope you didn't use all my hot water while you were butchering *Madame Butterfly*."

David sat down beside her and very lightly laid his open hand on her cheek. "Are you sore?"

"David!"

"Make you speechless, do I? That's what happens when a poor, confused woman finally has a good man take over. Now about our wager..."

Chelsea gave him a brooding look. "It was an accident, a freak of nature, a mistake, an aberration, a—"

"All that?" David whistled. "My, I guess I'll just have to keep convincing you, then." He leaned down to kiss her. "You wouldn't say I'm—we're—the greatest thing since sliced bread?"

"That really pleases your male ego, doesn't it?"

"Forget ego. You pleased other things much more. Do you have any idea how astonished you looked when you, shall we say, let go? Or when I made you let go, I guess."

"An aberration," Chelsea said, eyeing him with deliberate dislike.

He sighed, his deft fingers gently stroking over her blanketed breast. "In that case, and in the interest of pure science—"

"I'm not using any birth control," Chelsea said.

David jerked back and frowned down at her. "I should have realized that, but I was too far gone on you last night. Do you want me to pay a visit to your friendly neighborhood pharmacy?"

Chelsea looked thoughtful. "I don't know. I remember overhearing one of my father's friends joking about wearing socks in the shower, and the guys he was talking to all groaned. Is it that bad?''

"No, not really, but I would prefer feeling you and just you, and me and just me."

His words evoked very specific images in her mind, and she was appalled to feel a spurt of warmth.

"I guess I would, too," she said in a low voice.

"Do you want me to go through the alternatives? With pros and cons?"

"No, I'll go see my gynecologist."

"Who is he?"

"He? No way. Maggie Smith is definitely a she. She's also George's doctor. Don't you remember? She delivered the Mallorys' perfect baby?"

"I remember. Forgive the brief short circuit." David arched a thick brow. "A woman doctor, huh? You mean you would have blown a fit in the emergency room if just any man had been there?"

"Probably not," she said honestly. "But you! That was very different, and you know it."

"Do you know that the gossip at the hospital is still rampant? I'll walk by doctors I barely know and they'll poke each other in the ribs and talk just loud enough for me to hear about The Lecher in the ER. You've made me a legend in my own time."

"Well, I think you proved it was true last night."

"As in a Mark I lecher?"

She felt his hand drift over her shoulders to stop just above her breast. "No," she said, smiling shyly up at him, "as in a David I lecher."

He felt absurdly pleased. "Will you describe my very manly technique in one of your novels?"

She tried to look uncertain, but couldn't quite manage it. She giggled. "Not until I'm certain it wasn't all a fluke."

He sighed deeply. "When can you get in to see Maggie?"

"Well, I suppose that if we must continue with the experiment, it had better be soon."

David sent devout thanks upward. "How about socks in the shower until then?"

"Do I have a choice?"

"Nope, not one. But you've got me."

"Did I ask for this?" Chelsea asked her bedroom.

"Well you did moan quite a bit, and make those cute little pleading sounds."

"Why don't you practice verbal abstinence for a bit?"

"Where's the nearest pharmacy?"

Chelsea moaned when his fingers finally stroked her. "You're a wretched tease," she gasped. "Men aren't supposed to tease."

"You're easy," David said, grinning even as he kissed her. "And here I thought men would be replaced by technology."

"Not yet," Chelsea said, and glided her own hand down over his stomach. When she felt his muscles tighten she said, "I might be easy, but I'm not simple."

He entered her powerfully, fully, and she watched the myriad expressions on his face as he moved over her. "You are so beautiful, David," she said, lurching more closely against him when his fingers found her.

"Moan for me, Chelsea," he said, and she did.

* * *

Chelsea found herself stunned three more times that weekend. In her novels lovemaking between the hero and heroine always got better, but she'd sincerely doubted that that was true in real life.

But it certainly seemed to be. It had to be the lost weekend, she thought.

"I love your belly," David said. "Almost as much as your bottom."

"You ain't so bad yourself, Doctor," she said, gazing at him pointedly.

Under her fond gaze he became quite enthusiastic. "You *are* a lecher," Chelsea said, laughing.

"I don't think that *lecher* fits my uptight, stuffed-shirt Bostonian image."

"You're becoming more Californian by the day. What an improvement!"

Suddenly David cursed.

"What's wrong with you?" Chelsea asked, her fingers busily kneading his shoulders.

"I'm out of socks," he said in a very mournful voice. "And I suppose I should get myself home. I'm on duty early tomorrow morning, and I definitely need to recharge my batteries with some uninterrupted sleep. I've got a staff meeting, and I've got to be brilliant."

"Want me to write a script for you?"

"As in how to cure atrophy and not through surgery?"

"How about acupuncture?"

"As in insertion of a needle or something a trifle more dramatic into a prescribed point in the body?"

"You're terrible, and not at all serious. I do think, Dr. Winter, that I could nibble your neck right now and talk Transylvanian, and you wouldn't mind at all."

"You want me to be laid back, do you?"

He kissed her goodbye for the dozenth time. "Try to see Maggie tomorrow, okay?"

"I certainly don't want to be responsible for impeding a scientific study," she said, shooting him an impish smile.

David discovered during the following weeks that he had, miraculously, become a toucher. If he was driving he held her hand. If they were watching TV he could never remember the plots because his hands were busily doing their own plotting.

"I need my Chelsea fix," he announced to himself one afternoon at the hospital. He hadn't seen her for two days. He wondered if he were going off the deep end. If he was, he decided, it was the greatest thing that had ever happened to him. Boston winters, very competitive professional people, stuffy parties—all seemed light-years away. But he missed his kids and worried about them. Damn, he didn't want them developing ulcers, and with the none-too-subtle pressure doubtless exerted on them, it could happen. He wanted them to be happy. He wanted them to be as carefree as their dear old dad was now.

He and Chelsea were dining out, David holding Chelsea's hand, his thumb stroking her palm, when he told her of his concern.

Chelsea was pleased, because David rarely spoke of his life in Boston. "There's competition out here, too, David. It's just that it's difficult to be totally immersed, as it were, when the weather is so enticing, and the ocean is at your back door, and everywhere you look it's like a postcard.''

"And the pace of things is slower. Even sick people don't seem quite as sick in the emergency room. A lot of the residents are uptight, of course, but they've got boards to worry about and higher ups to impress.''

"Tell me about medical school.''

David groaned. "I worked my butt off.''

"The original overachiever, huh?''

"That was just part of it.''

"But there are rewards to being a doctor.''

"True, and I firmly believe that after four years of university, four years of medical school, a year of internship and up to five years of residency, there should be something. Hell, Chels, the long hours don't magically stop after residency. They never stop. Most doctors I know deserve their income, and they really care about their profession and doing the right thing for their patients. I shudder to think about socialized medicine taking hold here in the U.S.''

"I agree that the foundation of our society—work hard, excel, and there's a payoff—shouldn't be tampered with. I suspect if the reward weren't there, the quality of service would fall.''

"Brilliantly put,'' David said, beaming at her. Of course, she'd spoken aloud his own thoughts on the subject. "Now that we've resolved that problem, what was that you were saying about dinner with the boys?''

"Not just Angelo, Maurice and Delbert. One of my writer friends from Sacramento, Cindy Wright, is coming. She used to live here in Sausalito, then moved. She breaks into wild sobs and deep sighs every time she comes back for a visit. She needs her Marin fix about every two weeks.''

"Is that as dramatic as my Chelsea fix?"

"Yes, but not in the same way."

"Does she have a mouth like yours?"

"You can count on that, Doctor!"

"Does she look like you too?"

"Well, as a matter of fact, a writer friend of Cynthia's told me back in New York that we looked like sisters. I was astounded, and so was Cynthia. We quickly realized that we'd just insulted each other and decided that sisters it would be."

"Ah, but her bottom? No one's bottom could be as delicious as yours."

"I don't think I'd be quite that specific with Cindy. She just might give you some socks for your birthday. Knitted."

Cindy, David quickly discovered, was a whirlwind who gave him a disconcerting look and thrust a champagne bottle at him. She was small, like Chelsea, with dark hair and sparkling eyes. He thought her delightful, and waited for the coming of the inevitable bedlam.

It started when he heard her say to Chelsea, "I never should have left! Do you think I should hang out at the hospitals in Sacramento? He's a hunk, Chels." He moved a bit closer when she lowered her voice. All he could make out was something about thick fingers and big toes . . .

Then Chelsea broke into merry laughter.

"All right, Cindy, time to check the board and carry out Sarah's instructions for dinner."

"This time," Cindy said firmly, "I'm going to make certain everything gets to the table at the same time, and hot. Remember that one banquet where you forgot to put in the main course?''

Besides Angelo, Maurice and Delbert, another man showed up, a journalist named John Sanchez. "He's into crime and erotic Marin scandals," Cindy told David by way of introduction. "He's usually harmless and reasonable, except for his refusal to wear the beautiful yellow sweater I bought him for Christmas last year."

"Hi," said John Sanchez, shaking David's hand. "I've got this problem and Chelsea told me I should ask you about it. Do you play chess?"

David, who had thought he'd be doling out medical advice, grinned. "I was pretty good until my brain cells started dying off."

John concentrated for a long moment on stuffing his pipe. "Chelsea gave me a beginners' chess book for my birthday, so I guess you must be better."

"Come on, boys and girls," Maurice called from the dining room table. "Let's get with it. We're allowing forty-five minutes for dinner. Then onward to poker. Delbert needs money for his gambling debts." He turned to Chelsea and continued without pause, "Well, sweetie, you look like a woman who's finally met her match."

"I don't smoke," Chelsea said.

"Lord that was bad," John said, sucking on his already dead pipe.

"Does he like racing?" Delbert asked. "I don't remember."

"He looks tired, Chelsea," Angelo said. "You're not overextending him, are you, dear?"

"More beer?" Chelsea asked the table at large.

"Champagne," Cindy said.

John Sanchez looked up and said, as he tapped his pipe into an ashtray, "Make that a Chi Chi, Chelsea. I want to drink to my mother."

"John!" Cynthia said, punching him in the arm. "Your mother's going to smack you if you keep accusing her of hanging out at the Polo Lounge!"

"She loves it," John said, eyeing Cynthia's bust swathed in a new yellow sweater with black swirls on it.

"Ah, lust at the dinner table," Maurice said.

Cynthia and John disappeared into the kitchen to get dessert. When they came out, Cindy called out, "Get the camera, Chels. This is our new routine."

"Sunglasses?" David said.

"Absolutely," Cindy said.

Chelsea got her camera and snapped some corker photos.

Maurice said to John, "You know, I've never met a Sanchez with blond hair before."

John stuffed his pipe and took three matches to light it. He said in a bland voice, between puffs, "It's in the genes. Actually, I used to be a bullfighter."

"Ha," said Cindy. "Actually, guys, Sanchez was only a cow fighter. And still is."

"Come on, John, tell the truth," Chelsea said. "All you ever did was try to kill your dog with a rake."

"Unjust, unfair," said John. He turned to David. "You wanna play chess while these thugs try to kill each other at poker?"

"No way," said Delbert firmly. "I want to win the doc's money. With David eyeing Chelsea like your raked dog with a meaty bone, he doesn't stand a prayer."

"John doesn't either," Cindy said. "Now, you guys, before the slaughter begins, we've got to write down our ratings for dinner on Sarah's board in the kitchen." The average rating for a delicious meal of chicken enchiladas, tacos, homemade salsa and re-fried beans, was a nine point five.

David, true to Delbert's prediction, got wiped out by ten o'clock. John was wiped out by eleven, and his pipe was nearly chewed through. He mumbled every once in a while that he preferred humiliation by chess. Cindy and Chelsea were attacking a bottle of white wine, and only laughed when Delbert showed a full house, reducing them to quarter chips.

"I thought Cindy was staying with you," David said when everyone trooped out thirty minutes later.

"And you were depressed, weren't you?"

"You got it, lady."

"Well, you're saved by John Sanchez. The two of them tape every movie in the world and spend hours in front of the tube, watching."

David pulled her into his arms and kissed the tip of her nose. "Is that all they do in front of the tube?"

"That, Doctor, you will have to ask them! My lips are sealed."

"I'll just have to take care of that, won't I?" David said, and began kissing her.

"You look like a very smug man," Elliot said to David one afternoon at the swimming pool. It was a week before Christmas, sixty-five degrees outside and sunny.

"Chelsea is the most unaccountable female," David said. "I swear, we argue as much as we love. At least it's never boring."

Elliot grinned. "George told me that Maggie called you with a full report on Chelsea when she went in for an exam."

"Yes," David said. "I've never been more embarrassed. That wouldn't happen in Boston."

"That's a pity," Elliot said. "She did the same thing to me when I sent George to her. When are you flying out?"

"In three days. Back to snow and ice and wind-chill factors. I think my blood's thinned out. I don't know if this poor body will be able to tolerate building a snowman with the kids this year."

But there was no snowman that year. One day before David planned to leave, he got a phone call at the hospital.

"I can't believe the hospital is the only place I can reach you, David."

David stared at the phone as if it were a piece of rare steak that had just walked off his plate. "Margaret?"

"Who else, darling? Is that laughter I hear in the background? In your precious, very serious hospital?"

"This is California, Margaret," he said to his exwife in a very tense voice. "Did you call for my flight schedule? The kids are okay, aren't they? And Mom and Dad?"

"No, dear, yes, and the same as ever. Merry Christmas, David. The kids and I are here, at your apartment. Your security guard let us in. When are you coming home?"

David closed his eyes for a moment, visions of utter disaster clashing in his numbed brain.

"David?"

"Tell the kids I'll be there in a couple of hours. I assume you've made yourself at home?"

"Certainly, David."

"Give the kids my love." He sat as still as a pet rock for several minutes after he hung up the phone.

"Are you all right, Dr. Winter?"

David stared silently at Elsa. "What? Oh, yeah, just fine. I feel like a termite on his way to extermination. I feel like the dog that John tried to rake. What's up?"

"Got a little girl with a severe laceration on her leg. Fell off her bike. The kid's being taken care of. It's the mother Dr. Fellson needs you for. The woman's an unholy terror and needs your diplomatic touch."

David wasn't free to call Chelsea for another two hours. When he did, there was no answer. He cursed at the ringing phone. He was supposed to have dinner at her house at seven o'clock. Their last night together until he got back from Boston. He thought of the 1935 *Debrett's* he'd found in the dirty recesses of a used-book store, what he had lovingly thought of as her eight-pound Christmas present.

It was wrapped in bright red paper at home, he realized, sitting in full sight of anyone who cared to look on his coffee table.

Chapter 10

Hello, Father."

"Hi, Dad."

The two young voices were restrained, and their owners stood at nervous attention, watching him. David felt an overflowing of intense love as he looked at his children. God, they'd grown, changed, and it had only been six months since he'd seen them. "Hi, guys," he said, his voice shaking just a bit. "How about a hug for dear old Dad?"

Taylor bounded toward him, snuck a look at her mother, slowed and allowed herself to be hugged heartily. She had just turned seven, and Mark, David knew, was wild to turn nine to keep a full two years between him and his sister. Taylor was tall, nearly as tall as her brother, and she looked like her father, bless her. Mark was more like Margaret, small boned, with light brown hair and blue eyes.

"Hello, son," David said, looking over Taylor's head. He enfolded the boy in his arms. For the first time in their lives he found himself noticing his children's lack of spontaneity, their lack of enthusiasm. Well, maybe it was natural. After all, he'd been out of their lives for a while now.

"You guys like the flight here?"

"Yes, Dad," Taylor said. "The flight attendant gave me three packets of peanuts."

"She gave two back, of course," Margaret Winter said. She nodded toward David. "You're looking fit. Children, go sit down. One shouldn't make noise in an apartment. It disturbs the other tenants."

"Yes, Mother," Mark said. "Come along, Taylor."

"It's a flat and the penthouse, Margaret. You make it sound like a tenement," David said, watching his two children march like little troopers into the living room. He frowned, already foreseeing those ulcers.

"Well, it isn't exactly a brownstone in Beacon Hill, is it?" She smiled brightly up at him, cleansing away the insult in her words.

He'd loved that house, but of course it had gone to her in the divorce settlement. He said nothing, merely shook his head, wanting to keep the peace. "Why did you come here with no warning, Margaret?"

"All their friends' parents decided to go to the south of France for Christmas. I thought it would be nice to see what all this is about."

"This? You mean beautiful California?"

"Why, yes. You're looking quite well, David."

"So are you, Margaret. That's a very becoming dress."

"You always were partial to clingy wool."

That was a conversation stopper for sure, and David merely nodded and walked into the living room.

"Dad," Taylor said, "this is a very heavy present. It's a book, isn't it? Who's it for?"

"For someone named Chelsea," Margaret said. "How bizarre."

"Bizarre? How's that?"

"As in a section of London. I've never known a Chelsea."

How could she make it sound like chopped liver? David wondered.

"*Is* it a book, Father?" Taylor asked again.

"Yes, punkin, it is. Actually, it's a book on British peerages and such."

"You mean like dukes and earls and Prince Charles?"

"Exactly. Would you guys like a soda?"

"They would prefer some hot chocolate, perhaps, but I couldn't find any of the ingredients," Margaret said.

"There's no sugar in the soda, Margaret. Let's keep their teeth healthy. Come along, guys, and let's see what I've got."

Taylor and Mark followed him sedately into the kitchen. They were dressed like little preppies, he saw, and winced. Taylor didn't drink soda out of a can. It had to be in a glass, with three ice cubes.

"Tell me what you've been up to the past six months," David said, seating himself at the kitchen table. For God's sake, he shouldn't be so ill at ease around his own children.

For the next ten minutes both children stumbled through a recital of events. "Of course," Mark concluded, "Mother didn't allow me to be in that play. It was far too plebeian."

Merciful heavens, David thought, he even pronounced the word correctly. He glanced up at the kitchen clock. Six.

"I would like to hear more," he said, rising. "We'll all go out to dinner at the Cliff House. It's a great place and you can see lots of seals from the window. Why don't you go get cleaned up? We'll leave in fifteen minutes."

"It sounds interesting, Father," Mark said.

No, David wanted to correct him, it sounded neat. "Interesting" was the response to a boring comment.

The only one left was Margaret. He said bluntly, as he walked into the living room, "I have one guest room, Margaret. Are you planning on sleeping with the kids?"

"No, I'll take the sofa."

"Why not a hotel? I can call if you like."

"No, here will be just fine."

He nodded, defeated, and said, "I've got a phone call to make and plans to break. Excuse me."

He listened to the third ring, then the fourth.... Then, "Hello!"

"Hi, Chels, David. Bad news, wretched news, ghastly and all that, except for my kids."

"All right, give."

"Margaret flew in with the children this afternoon. They're all here at my place, and I'm tied up. I can't make tonight. I'm sorry."

Chelsea looked at her romantically set table. "Me, too," she said on a sigh. "Well, at least you won't be going out of town, and I'll be able to meet your kids."

"Well, yes. Let me see what I can work out."

"David?"

"Yes?"

"You won't believe your Christmas present." She giggled.

"Well, you won't be able to lift yours!"

"A big red bow around your middle? Maybe an apple in your mouth?"

He laughed. "Not this year, maybe next. Or your birthday. I'll talk to you tomorrow, Chels."

Chelsea hung up the phone, a thoughtful expression on her face. Unexpected. She found herself wondering why Margaret had come out without warning. Refusing to follow that train of thought, Chelsea finally snuggled up with a Dorothy Garlock novel, remembering how she'd joked with Dorothy in New York about the second word of her two-word title—Lash! Ah, what marvelous images that evoked. Great novel, she thought, finishing about midnight. Because she didn't want to brood, she dove into the history of medicine she'd found for her doctor, Saint, in her San Francisco novel.

The evening wasn't exactly a bust, David told himself as he settled down to sleep. The kids hadn't loosened up, but he knew he had to be patient. It occurred to him that their formal behavior had been the acceptable norm during his marriage to Margaret. Had he really been such a stuffed shirt? So cold and... rigid? As for Margaret, she'd been pleasant, quite pleasant, in fact. Still, it was going to be difficult living with her until—until when? He hadn't asked her how long she intended to stay. Indeed, his thinking continued, it would be quite nice if she could take herself back to Boston and leave the kids with him for the remainder of their vacation. He decided to discuss it with her in the morning.

He didn't have the chance.

Margaret announced over a delicious breakfast that she herself had prepared, "David, you will have the children to yourself today. I have errands to run. Will that be all right with you?"

What errands? he wondered, but said nothing. "Certainly."

David thoughtfully finished his pancakes, making his decision just as Margaret emerged from the bathroom, looking exquisitely lovely.

"Well," she said, "I'll be off now. I rented a car, David, so you don't have to worry about driving me about. Now, children, I expect you to do as your father says. All right?"

"Yes, Mother."

"Yes, ma'am."

She kissed them both, nodded to David and left.

David looked at his children. He believed at that moment that he could count the number of days on his left hand that he'd spent with them, alone, just the three of them. He realized that he had no idea what to do with them. Well, it was time he learned how to be a father.

He took his two little Bostonian preppies to the De Young Museum in Golden Gate Park. He decided, after three hours, that he was enjoying it more than they were. The children didn't eat junk food, as they succinctly informed him, so he trotted them to Fisherman's Wharf for some fresh seafood.

He stared out over the Bay as he ate his shrimp salad, his eyes resting on the sailboats. That's it! He'd take them sailing.

"Kids," he said, "how would you like to go out on my sailboat this afternoon?"

Taylor looked at Mark, a silent message passing between them. "That would be very pleasant, Father," Taylor said.

Yeah, David thought. You sound about as excited as if I'd offered you a live squid.

Chelsea, he thought, and smiled. She loved to sail. He kept his fingers crossed that she'd be free and willing as he excused himself and phoned her.

The outing sounded great to Chelsea, so David was driving over the Golden Gate Bridge some thirty minutes later.

Chelsea, dressed in her grubby sailing togs, answered the doorbell, a wide smile on her face. The smile cracked when she observed the two children flanking David. Sailing, she thought. Is he out of his mind? Both children were dressed like little fashion plates.

"Hello," she said, stepping back. "Come in. I'm Chelsea." The children filed in, stopped and turned.

"I'm Taylor."

"I'm Mark."

"And I'm David."

"And I'm overwhelmed! Come on in and sit down. What can I get you guys to drink?"

"A club soda," Taylor said.

"A root beer," Mark said.

"A stiff scotch," David said.

Chelsea shot him a wicked look and went into the kitchen. As she was making up the order she heard Taylor say, "Father, she's got a patch on her jeans!"

"A patch on her bottom," Mark said, a fiend for specificity.

David wanted to groan. He looked at his kids, really looked at them, and realized that the last thing they could do was go sailing in the ridiculous outfits they were wearing. And he wasn't much better, for God's sake. Slacks and a sport jacket!

"Her jeans are very tight," Taylor said. "Mother says that girls should never wear clothes that are too tight. They're not—"

She broke off as Chelsea came back into the living room.

I should have waited, Chelsea thought, smiling to herself. She would have liked to hear about too tight clothes and what the great Margaret had to say about them. And, she thought, my jeans aren't too tight.

"You know my father?" Mark asked, sipping his root beer, eyeing this woman whose black hair was bouncing all over her head.

Chelsea's eyes twinkled. "Yes," she said, "I guess I do know him, a bit."

"How long have you known my father?" Taylor asked.

"Not as long as I've known Torquemada," Chelsea said.

"Torque-who?" Mark asked.

"He was a very famous fellow who loved to ask people questions," Chelsea said.

"Oh," Mark said.

If the preceding minutes could have been called a conversation, there was a definite pregnant silence now.

Chelsea continued after a pained moment to Mark. "This fellow, Torquemada, if he didn't like the answers he got to his questions, he pulled out the person's fingernails." She splayed her fingers. "He wouldn't have had much luck with me, as you can see."

"Do you bite your fingernails?" Taylor asked, her voice a mixture of distaste and fascination.

"Only if I get mad at them," Chelsea said. "Actually, I type a lot and have to keep them short."

"You're a secretary?" Taylor asked, obviously horrified.

Chelsea cocked her head. Bloody little snob, she thought. David looked embarrassed. "And if I were, Taylor?"

Taylor realized she'd insulted an Adult and quickly retrenched. "Mother says that ladies don't work."

"And how about gentlemen?" Chelsea asked.

"That's different," Mark said.

"Why?"

David cleared his throat, wishing he'd never come up with this doomed idea. Before he could extricate everyone from this morass, Taylor said primly, "Grandmother Winter says that a lady is best served by allowing her husband to take care of her."

Dear heavens, Chelsea thought, that sounded like a recording! How ghastly! "How old is Grandmother Winter?"

"Old," said Mark.

"Her hair is silver," said Taylor.

"I suppose that's a step up from blue," Chelsea said.

"It is bluish," Taylor said.

Chelsea wanted a glass of white wine.

"Are you a secretary?" Taylor asked again.

"Tenacious, aren't you?" Chelsea replied.

"It's too bad you don't have a gentleman to take care of you," Mark said. "But your house is nice."

It's time to intervene, David decided at that last note of childish candor. "Chelsea is a lady, kids, and she isn't a secretary, she's a novelist. She writes books. Is that acceptable?" he added, his voice just a bit sharp.

Round, astonished eyes regarded Chelsea.

"Real books?" Taylor said.

"With covers and pictures?" Mark said.

"With sexy plots?" David said.

"Even with words and titles," Chelsea said, and burst into laughter.

"So that's why Dad bought you—"

"That's a surprise, Mark," David said quickly.

Children, Chelsea thought a moment later. What an odd experience, for sure. She rose. "Now, you guys, neither of you would last three minutes on a sailboat. You'd skitter off the deck with those shoes. Your father isn't in much better shape, either. Tell you what let's do, instead. Sausalito is a marvelous place to explore. We can do some shopping and feed the sea gulls and stuff ourselves with cookies."

Their eyes turned toward David.

"Sounds great to me."

They watched the ferry dock, wandered through the touristy shops and fed the sea gulls. "All right, sport," Chelsea said, turning to David. "Give me one of your credit cards. Taylor and I are going in this boutique and you, my dear, can take Mark shopping. This will be expensive, but, after all, you *are* a gentleman, and all of us are in need of care."

Both children looked dubious.

"David," Chelsea added just before they split up, "grubby stuff, okay?" She added to Mark, "Sailing is a messy business, but somebody has to do it."

"Now, Taylor, come with me. Meet you all back here in one hour!"

Taylor giggled at her image in the mirror. She was wearing prewashed jeans and a Sausalito sweatshirt. Pink sneakers were on her small feet.

The immense cost of looking casually grubby, Chelsea thought as she signed David's name to the credit card slip.

"What do you think, Taylor?"

"I think," Taylor said, her young voice suddenly very serious, "that Mother wouldn't like it."

"In that case," Chelsea said, "you can leave your things at my house. You ready to do a cartwheel for your dad?"

Margaret dropped her bomb the following afternoon. They'd just returned from Chinatown, and the kids' feet hurt from walking up and down all the hills. David wished he'd brought their sneakers home from Chelsea's house for them. Margaret looked as unmussed and immaculate as usual. "Children," Margaret said, "I want you to go into your room and play with the puzzle I bought you."

"Regular little soldiers, Margaret," David said.

"They mind," Margaret said. "And so should all children."

"I suppose so," David said wearily. "It's just that they don't seem to have as much life in them as before."

"How would you know about that? Did you expect them to hang about your neck with joy? You were home so rarely, after all."

He wanted to retort with something suitably snide, but there was a lot of truth to what she said. He'd wanted to avoid her, and thus had also avoided his children.

Margaret continued after a moment, her voice very matter-of-fact. "I'm delighted your attitude had become more parental—"

"What the hell do you expect? I love them, Margaret!"

"Yes, of course you do," she said in a surprisingly gentle voice.

He stared at her, then frowned. "All right. What's up?"

"He's a general in the army and I want to fly to Honolulu to see him."

"What?"

"His name is General Nathan Monroe, and I met him at a party in Boston. He's a very nice man, a widower, and I want to spend some time with him. That's why I brought the children here, to you."

She's acting like a child who needs her parents' permission, David thought blankly, staring at his ex-wife. Did she believe he would have refused her if she'd called with her plans before flying out?

"That's great," he said for want of anything better. A general, for God's sake! He pictured his children goose-stepping, then chided himself for being ridiculous.

"How long do you plan to stay in Honolulu?"

He watched, fascinated, as a flush spread over her cheeks. It brought back an ancient memory. Before they were married, he'd asked her to spend the weekend with him at the Cape. Hadn't she flushed then, just as now? And she'd said yes then, too.

"Actually," Margaret said calmly, "Nathan and I plan to spend a week in Honolulu, then a couple of days on Maui. Then we play to fly to Washington to spend a couple of days with his daughter and son. I was hoping you wouldn't mind if the children accompanied us to Washington."

"I see," David said. "That will be fine, of course."

"If it's all right with you, David," she continued, "I should like to meet this Chelsea person. Mark mentioned that he'd never met a lady like her before. Taylor said she wrote books. Is she a proper person for them to know? Or is she very . . . California?"

"What exactly does that mean?" he said.

Margaret shrugged. "Well, I'm not really certain. Being from California brings a certain *image* to mind, I suppose. Hippies and drugs and all that."

"Margaret, that was back in the sixties."

"No need to raise your voice, David. If you aren't concerned about the type of person you introduce our children to, I am. It's important that they aren't exposed to any bad influences."

He could only stare at her. He said finally, "Chelsea Lattimer isn't a type, Margaret. She is, as a matter of fact, a very loving, warm person, who also just happens to be very talented."

"What type of books does she write?" Margaret asked.

"Long historical novels," David said absently. Then he smiled. "They're the ones with the wild covers, filled with adventure, romance and intrigue."

"Good heavens," Margaret said suddenly, "I thought her name sounded familiar! I've seen her books, if one could call them books!" She shuddered. "Not exactly biographies of Winston Churchill, are they?"

"No, and I imagine that she sells a good deal better," David retorted. "Her novels are not only well written and historically accurate, they're excellent escapism, just downright fun, as a matter of fact."

"Yes, certainly you're right." Margaret turned toward the window, saying over her shoulder, "As I recall, you don't approve of women who are, shall we say, independent, out on their own, without male protection. It surprises me that you would see a woman who is that way."

There was a brief, pained silence. Was I really such a jerk? David was asking himself. Out of self-protection, he didn't decide at that moment on an answer.

"I gather she makes a good deal of money?"

"I don't know what she makes. It's none of my business, but I should say that she does quite well."

Where the hell is all this leading? David wondered. All too soon he discovered the circuitous direction of Margaret's thinking.

Chapter 11

Have you met the Winston-Barnetts?" Margaret asked, turning from the window to face him.

"Certainly," David said. "Mr. Winston-Barnett—Andrew, I believe—is a broker on Wall Street, isn't he?" At Margaret's nod he said, "And he has a son and daughter. Why do you ask?"

"His daughter, Andrea, is now living here, in San Francisco."

"So?"

"As you know, she and I went to school together, at Vassar. She's a widow now, but her husband left her quite well off. I thought it would be . . . kind of you to see her."

David pictured an Andrea of nearly ten years before. Tall, very Nordic-looking, with pale blond hair and light blue eyes. He said only, "I seem to remember her."

"She, of course, doesn't write books or anything like that, but she has our—your—background, David. She admitted to me a few months ago that she would very much like to see you. After her husband's death she went back to her maiden name."

"Must take up a lot of space on a check," David said.

"She is a very well-bred, lovely lady," Margaret said, keeping her temper in check. One could never tell with David. Particularly since he'd left Boston. She did not appreciate unpredictability. It was, in fact, rather annoying. Thank heaven Nathan was enchantingly predictable.

"I'm certain she is," David said. "Honestly, Margaret, this sounds perilously close to wife swapping!"

"Her husband died in a plane crash," Margaret said. "There is no swapping involved, David."

"Why the devil is she interested in seeing me?"

"She has always admired you," Margaret said, her voice cool now, her tone denying that she approved of this idea. "As I said, she is also financially independent, just as your... friend is."

"Can it, Margaret," David said. "I have no interest in Andrea. I never did. If I recall correctly, she appeared about as warm as a fish that had been on ice for six months."

"She doesn't wallow in things like that," Margaret said, her cheeks flushing just a bit, not with embarrassment, but with anger. "If sex is what you're referring to."

David grinned; he couldn't help himself. Then he laughed. "I don't suppose you told her that I was a sex fiend?"

"I expected that you'd gotten over that some years ago. At least, you did with me."

"It isn't that I got over it," David said, still chuckling. "It's just that I gave up on you. Incidentally, just how old is this general fellow? Perhaps he's given up on sex?"

"Nathan," Margaret said stiffly, "is a gentleman. He is very concerned for *my* feelings, and he isn't old, David."

Oh, Margaret, David thought, looking at his ex-wife. We certainly didn't do things right, did we? He said abruptly, closing the subject, "I wish you luck with your gentleman general, Margaret. And I am sorry, but Andrea Winston-Barnett will have to fend for herself." He added, lightly touching her arm, "You've done your duty, but I'm really not at all interested."

"I suppose this Chelsea woman gives you all the sex you want?"

"Didn't you see the gray hairs?" he asked, trying to keep things light.

"I thought as much," Margaret said distastefully, moving away from him. "Since she doesn't appear to be after you for your money, she must be one of those loose individuals that sleep from pillar to post."

"What an odd phrase," David said, but he felt his hands clenching at his sides. He saw that she was revved up for more insults and said quickly, "Let's drop it, all right, Margaret? I imagine the children have done the puzzle, probably two times over by now."

"Very well," Margaret said stiffly, and walked toward the door.

"Margaret," he called after her quietly. She turned. "Did you ever think I was sexy? Did you ever enjoy making love with me?"

"Yes," she said just as quietly. "And yes." She turned again and left the living room.

Life, he thought, staring after her, is bloody strange.

Dr. Harold Lattimer put down the phone and looked at his wife. "It appears that our little girl has gotten herself into it this time," he said, shaking his head.

"David Winter is a fine man," Mimi said. "I wish the lot of them could come here for Christmas. This will be the first year Chelsea hasn't been home."

"I wonder if she would have come if his children hadn't been dropped on his doorstep?"

Mimi tried for a Gaelic shrug, her memory of Paris still warm. *"Qui sait?"* she asked. She frowned a moment, wondering if that was correct, then shrugged again. It sounded good, and it sounded French.

Dr. Lattimer reached for the phone.

"Who are you calling, Harry?"

"A catering company in Marin," he said. "I'll have them make up a big Christmas feast for Chelsea and her brood. I don't think Chelsea would know the front end of a turkey from its pope's nose."

"I say, Harry," Mimi said after he'd made the catering arrangements, "I could get us two tickets for, say, London."

"Look," he grumbled, "they do speak English there, but it just isn't proper English."

"I have it, then," Mimi announced. "Hawaii!"

Harry Lattimer knew when he'd lost. He had no hope at all that there wouldn't be reservations available, even at this late date. Mimi *always* got reservations.

Chelsea placed the phone back into its cradle and stared for a moment at absolutely nothing. Her first exposure to David's children hadn't been a particularly startling success. Christmas was, for Chelsea, a time of laughter and fun, not two blank-faced kids sitting on the edge of the sofa, staring at her as if she were the wicked witch of the West, bent on hexing their father.

When a messenger had delivered a cuckoo clock later that afternoon, wrapped in a huge red bow, and a notice that her Christmas meal for four people would be catered, she laughed so hard it took a rude noise from the messenger to get his tip.

"George," she said into the phone a few minutes later, "you're simply not going to believe what my folks have done now!"

"Knowing your parents, Chels, it has to be outrageous," George said, rearranging Alex on her shoulder. "Come on, give."

"A cuckoo clock and a catered Christmas meal for me, David and his kids! I do wonder what they meant by the cuckoo clock, though."

George dutifully laughed, then said, "That takes care of Christmas Day. How 'bout the group of you coming here for dinner on Christmas Eve? I swear Elliot will do most of the cooking."

"You're not going to see your parents this year?"

"January will be our month for pilgrimages."

"It will be a madhouse," Elliot said later that evening after George gave him the news. "No," he amended thoughtfully, "probably not."

"Why not?"

"David's kids. They're so uptight, so very careful, you wonder if they ever fight, even between themselves."

"You've met them?"

"Yep. David brought them to the hospital for a tour. They were dressed like two little models, and so polite it made you nervous."

"What about their mother? Margaret, isn't that it?"

"The ex-Mrs. Winter has taken off for Honolulu to vacation with a general, so David said. Three stars. Most interesting."

George looked thoughtfully at the overly large serving Elliot had dished up for her dinner. "Chelsea is the unknown factor here, isn't she?"

"Eat," Elliot said automatically. "Do you wonder if those kids of David's can maintain their formal pose around her?"

"It is an interesting thought," said George.

Chelsea drove over the Golden Gate Bridge late on the afternoon of Christmas Eve, the passenger seat loaded with presents.

For once she wasn't plotting. She'd left her hero, Saint, blinded by an explosion at a foundry, and her heroine, Juliana, holding his head in her lap.

She stopped gnawing on her thumbnail long enough to pay her dollar toll.

"Merry Christmas," the fellow at the tollgate said.

"Yeah, Christmas," she said toward the presents beside her. She hadn't seen David or his children since that afternoon two days before, and she wondered how he was making out. On the phone he sounded

quite chipper, particularly since Margaret had left for
Hawaii. And, she thought, smiling a bit wickedly, he
missed her; that had been expressed in the most
mournful voice she'd ever heard from him.

She missed him, too. *I think I've become addicted
to him,* she admitted to herself as she turned her car
onto Lombard Street. She'd never been addicted to
anything before, certainly not a man, and it was a dis-
turbing thing to have happen.

She pulled into the driveway, noticed David's Lancia, Nancy, already parked on the sidewalk and
checked her face in the mirror. She was dressed to the
teeth, and was even wearing her lucky gray fedora. At
least it smashed down her hair a bit. "I look great,"
she told herself, "and there isn't a patch on my bottom."

David's eyes agreed with her own assessment. As for
her, she wanted to throw her arms around him and kiss
him until he was unconscious. Instead she said, "Hi."

"Hi, yourself, gorgeous," he said, and lightly kissed
her lips. "Lord, you smell good enough to eat," he
added.

She slanted him a look that made his body react instantly. "Chels," he said, and quickly turned away.

Taylor and Mark were seated just as she'd expected
them to be, stiff as little sticks on the edge of the sofa.
They greeted her politely, and that was that.

"White wine, please, Elliot," she whispered as he
hugged her. "A glass followed by a jug, probably."

"They'll loosen up, Chels," Elliot said. "Just be
yourself. No one can be immune to that."

Chelsea, fortified with a glass of white wine, joined
David and the kids.

"Dad took us to the hospital," Mark said.

"It smelled," Taylor said. "Very funny."

"I agree," Chelsea said. "I was there not too long ago and your dad took care of me. In a manner of speaking," she added, smiling crookedly at David.

"She was a lousy patient," David said. "Wouldn't do a thing I said, fought with me, yelled at me—"

"Goodness," Taylor said, wide-eyed. "You did that to Father?"

"He really isn't the pope, Taylor," Chelsea said. "There is bull involved, but there's nothing papal about it."

"You've been wrong before, Chels," David said, giving her an intimate look. "Remember?"

Chelsea sighed deeply. "No, not really. It's been too long."

"When were you wrong, Chelsea?" Mark asked.

"Well," Chelsea said confidentially, leaning toward Mark, "your father made me a wager. He took great advantage of me, I fear, but the results are still far from conclusive."

"I don't know about that," David began, only to leap to his feet when George, her timing always exquisite, came into the living room, carrying Alex.

"Oh," Taylor gasped, staring at the vision. "You're so beautiful!"

And what am I? Chelsea wondered. A witch with spinach between her teeth?

"Thank you," George said, smiling at the young girl. "You're Taylor, right? Mark? Welcome to our home. My name is George."

"That's a funny name," Mark said.

"Yes, very true. And this is Alex." She lowered the baby for inspection.

"He's awfully small," Taylor said. Alex, demonstrating a sudden burst of showmanship, grabbed her finger and gave her a blurred baby's smile.

"Yes, he is," George said. "It scares the wits out of me—you know, I'm afraid of dropping him on his head or something equally awful."

"Mother must have dropped you on your head," Mark said to his sister.

Excellent, Chelsea thought, they aren't always so saintly. She said to Taylor, "Do you know that George is a very famous model? She's also on TV."

"Really?" Taylor breathed reverently.

"Really," George said. "Would you like to hold Alex, Taylor?"

"You can pretend you're one of the Three Wise...women," Chelsea said.

George laughed. "He is perfect, Chels, but even I wouldn't go that far!"

"Dinner," Elliot said, coming into the living room. "I've done my best, guys. Hope you like everything."

Mark looked at Taylor, then blurted out, "You cooked dinner, sir?"

"Yes, indeed, Mark," Elliot said.

"But men don't do things like that," Taylor said.

"Are we going to have another truism from Grandmother Winter?" Chelsea asked.

"Yes," Taylor said firmly. "It is a woman's job to make the house pleasant and to manage the servants."

Elliot sent David a wicked, crooked grin, and David, wishing he could stuff cotton into Taylor's small mouth, hastily said, "Things are different in California, kids. Here men and women both do everything. It's . . . well, it's more fun that way."

"And we don't starve," George added. "Come into the dining room now. I'll put Alex to bed and join you shortly."

"Do you believe that, David?" Chelsea asked as they walked behind the kids into the dining room.

"I'm trying to figure out just what I believe," he said. "Odd, but I don't remember my mother being so very ironclad in her notions."

"You were a boy," Chelsea said, "not a girl."

He looked thoughtful at that. "I'll have to look after Taylor," he said. "Maybe it's not such a bad idea to have a woman bringing in the bread."

"Half a loaf," Chelsea said. "Less pressure on the husband, I expect."

"As in no ulcers?"

She merely smiled up at him, and he wanted at that instant to throw her to the floor and make love to her. He groaned softly, his hand on her back drifting lower for a moment.

His hand was just about to curve around her bottom, when he cursed softly and helped her into her chair. She heard Elliot chuckle.

Mark was uncertain whether he should compliment a man on his cooking. He was saved possible embarrassment when his dad said, "Great, Elliot. That dressing had cranberries and walnuts in it, right?"

Mark decided to be impressed. His dad knew the ingredients, so it must be all right, a manly thing, in fact. "Yes," he added, "and the gravy was wonderful."

"Thank you all," Elliot said. "Taylor, you want some more lemonade?"

"No, sir," Taylor said, sleepy from all the food.

George said, "Then why don't we all adjourn to the living room, drink some of Elliot's famous egg nog—two varieties—and open our presents?"

The adults' egg nog had enough whiskey to make an elephant dance, Chelsea thought after one mug. She looked at the children and saw their eyes fastened on the presents.

"My thought exactly," she said, and fished out a wrapped package addressed to Taylor. "It's from me," she said. "And here's yours, Mark."

She saw Taylor start to rip open the paper, then pause and, as if through sheer willpower, sedately begin to untie the ribbon.

I've got to do something about that, she thought. She found she was holding her breath as Taylor opened her box first.

"Oh!" Taylor said. She held up a huge panda bear and stared at it. There was a white bow around the bear's neck and an envelope attached. Taylor looked toward Chelsea, a question in her eyes.

"They're tickets to the zoo to see the pandas next week. They're here on loan from China."

To Chelsea's surprise, Taylor rose from her chair, walked to where Chelsea sat and kissed her cheek. "I've never had a bear before. Thank you."

"You're most welcome, Taylor. Now you, Mark."

Mark squealed; there was no other word for it. He gazed in reverent awe at the baseball and mitt, autographed by Tod Hathaway, George's brother. "Oh, Dad! Oh, goodness! Look!"

"My brother Tod," George said, "is the pitcher for the Oakland A's. He told me to tell you hello and to get out there and play."

The children's faces were lit up almost as brightly as the Christmas tree, and Chelsea felt David's eyes on her. She turned to see a very tender look and swallowed a bit.

"You hit the jackpot, Chels," he said, reaching out his hand to her. She took it, and he pulled her down beside him on the floor.

David gave Chelsea her *Debrett's*, and she squealed as loudly as Mark had. "I've always had to go to the library and breathe in endless amounts of dust," she said, so delighted that she kissed him on the mouth. She heard Taylor make a distressed sound and released him. "Thank you, David. It's a marvelous present. As for yours," she continued, lowering her voice a bit, "you'll have to wait until we're alone."

David groaned.

"The evening was quite a hit," David told her later as he walked her to her car. "Thanks for thinking of the kids."

"My pleasure," she said, looking up at him.

"Sometime soon, I hope," he said, and pulled her into his arms. "Your pleasure, that is." He kissed her deeply and sighed with his own pleasure at the feel of her bottom in his hands. He held her very close, then, with a sigh of regret, released her. "You sober enough to get home in one piece?"

"If I don't make it, it will be because of my lascivious thoughts and not the egg nog."

"Just hold those thoughts, sweetheart." He kissed her again and helped her into her car.

"Tomorrow, at about one o'clock, for our catered dinner," Chelsea said. "Starve the kids. There'll probably be enough goodies for an entire battalion."

David drove his very contented children home some minutes later. When he tucked them in Taylor gazed up at him with her owlish, candid look and said, "I saw you kissing Chelsea, Dad."

"Me, too," said Mark from the other bed.

"It is Christmas," David said, looking from one of his children to the other. "Goodwill and cheer and all that."

"You kissed her hard, Dad," Taylor said.

"And I saw your hands on her bottom before George yanked me away from the window."

"Just checking for patches?"

"Dad!"

"All right, you two, yes, I was kissing Chelsea. I like her very much."

"Are you going to marry her Dad?" Mark asked, adjusting the baseball and mitt on the pillow beside him.

David blinked at that.

"I sure like my panda," Taylor said.

If the two little devils could be bought, David thought, Chelsea had made a fine beginning. He said finally, his voice thoughtful, "You know, I doubt that Chelsea would want to marry me."

"Impossible!"

"Dad, you're the best in the world!"

Best at what? he wondered, kissing his daughter good-night.

He rose, then bent down to kiss Mark. When he straightened he said only, "Let's not discuss heavy stuff like that, okay? To be honest, guys, I have no idea what's going to happen."

As he walked out of the darkened bedroom he heard Taylor mutter to Mark, "I wonder if Mom is going to marry the general."

"I don't like it," Mark said.

Like which? David wondered as he quietly shut the door. The general or Chelsea?

Chapter 12

That was delicious prime rib, Chelsea," David said, sitting back in his chair, his hands on his stomach. "Death from pigdom is imminent."

"Me, too," Chelsea said. "How 'bout you guys?"

"That was as good as Dr. Mallory's dinner," Taylor said. "Thank you."

"Did men make this dinner, too," asked Mark.

"No, sir," Chelsea said. "This was the proud result of women's work. Not bad, huh?"

"Yummy," said Taylor. She'd brought her panda, and it was seated in its own chair. Its name was MacEnroe.

Chelsea regarded her stuffed guests with a smile that turned to a frown as she gazed out the window. It was raining in Marin on Christmas Day. All her plans for sailing, well...

"Housebound, I fear," David said, following her thinking. Then he gave her the most lecherous look she'd ever seen, and she threw up her hands, giggling.

"Was that a joke, Dad?" Mark asked, looking from one adult to the other.

David gave a wrenching sigh. "Actually not, Mark. Tell you what, kids, why don't I show a movie for you guys on Chelsea's VCR?"

"We don't watch TV during the day, Dad," Taylor said, her voice just a bit mournful.

"This is Christmas. You can do anything you want."

After settling the kids in front of the TV, David joined Chelsea in the kitchen. He stood in the doorway a moment, watching her. She was wearing gray wool slacks and a matching cashmere sweater. The slacks slithered delightfully over her bottom. "Well," he said, coming up behind her and kissing the back of her neck, "one should be able to do anything one wants on Christmas."

Chelsea felt a surge of warmth at the touch of his mouth, and frowned at the leftover green beans. He'd just kissed her neck, for heaven's sake, and here she was ready to attack him. She turned slowly, carefully set down the green beans and hugged him. "Merry Christmas, David," she said, and stood on her tiptoes to be kissed.

"You would make a turnip horny," he said after a moment.

"You are so romantic."

"I am right now in transition between a Mark I hero and a Mark II. It sometimes leads to misinterpretations of my deepest, most sincere thoughts and desires."

"That, David Winter, makes no sense at all. And there's not much to misinterpret about a turnip."

He kissed the tip of her nose, then held her against him a moment, just savoring her closeness, her warmth. "My kids informed me last night that they saw me kissing you *hard* before George yanked them away from the window."

"How did you slither out of that one?"

"It was tough, particularly when they pointed out that I was touching your bottom, too."

"Oh, dear," Chelsea said, pulling back from him just a bit. "If I recall correctly, that was my fault. I can't seem to keep my hands off you. Or stop encouraging you. Our scientific research and all that."

"I didn't keep any notes," David said, kissing her ear. "I think I've forgotten all the groundwork we laid."

"Laid? Really, doctor! Ah, but you still have the greatest enthusiasm," she said, feeling him hard against her belly.

He moaned deep in his throat, cupped her bottom in his hands and drew her up against him.

"Dad, do you think I—"

He released her very slowly before turning to his son. "Yes, Mark?"

"I—I'm sorry," Mark stammered. "I just wanted a glass of soda." His eyes went from his father's face to Chelsea's. "You were kissing again," he said.

"Yes," David said. "Yes, we were. A soda you say? Does Taylor want anything to drink?"

"No," Mark said, looking guilty. Chelsea wondered just how long the boy had been watching them before saying anything. She pulled herself together and said brightly, "You don't want to miss any of the movie, Mark. Go back in the living room and I'll bring you some root beer, okay?''

Mark nodded, but his gaze was searching and uncertain. Chelsea sighed. Play it light, she said to herself. You have no idea what David thinks or wants. She reminded herself to tell him how coincidental it was that her hero designations had the same name as his son. Maybe in the year 2000 his son would be a Mark III.

It wasn't difficult to be light and amusing during their late afternoon game of Trivial Pursuit. David had bought them the children's edition, and they switched back and forth from the children's to the adults'. Chelsea and Taylor were partners against the *men*.

Taylor, it turned out, was fantastic with the entertainment questions, Chelsea's inevitable Waterloo. They won, leading to the men's grousing and complaining about hard questions and general unluckiness with the dice.

"You're pretty smart," Taylor said as they prepared to leave that evening.

"That sounds like a judgment call," Chelsea said, ruffling Taylor's hair. "And oh, so true. You ain't bad yourself, kiddo."

"Mark said you and Dad were kissing again in the kitchen."

"Yes, your father is a very nice and kissable man."

"Mark also said Dad was holding your bottom again."

"That's possible, I guess."

"Are you going to marry my father?"

"That, Taylor, is a question I have no answer to, or to which I have no answer. Interesting syntax. Hmm.

And actually, I haven't the foggiest notion! Now you don't need that Boston coat or those ghastly boots. Just your sweater. The weather person said sun tomorrow. You want to go sailing?"

Marry David, Chelsea thought some thirty minutes later as she sat alone on her sofa, staring at the blank TV screen. Chelsea Lattimer Winter. CLW. Stop it, idiot! Just because you want to attack him physically every time you're around him—well, maybe that will go away. Most likely it will go away. Or hang around, like fungus or mold.

I am not a slice of bread!

"Oh, this is ridiculous!" Chelsea said, and went to bed.

She picked up one of Laura Parker's novels, *Rose of the Mists*, and reread it until three o'clock in the morning.

They made it to the sailboat, got the lunch stowed below and the sails ready to raise, when David's beeper went off.

Chelsea jumped.

She knew David wanted to curse but restrained himself in front of the kids. He smiled, a forced motion of muscles, and said, "Let me go call in. It's probably nothing. I'll be right back."

"This wouldn't happen if he was visiting in Boston," Mark said.

"Yeah," Taylor said. "They couldn't beep him that far away."

Both Taylor and Mark were dressed in their casual togs David and Chelsea had bought them in Sausalito. Now they both looked utterly disconsolate.

Chelsea cleared her throat. "Mark, go below and get some bread. We'll feed the gulls until your father gets back."

This occupation hadn't paled by the time David returned, but the look on his face paled everything.

He said tersely, "There's been a huge accident on 101. I've got to go in now."

Actually, Chelsea had already made up her mind, given this contingency. "Give me the boat keys, David. I'll take the kids out."

David looked uncertain. Two children who could fall overboard in two seconds and one very small woman whose skill at sailing was undoubtedly excellent, but still . . .

"Key, please, David," Chelsea said. "It will be all right."

"Please, Dad!"

"Chelsea knows everything, Dad."

"No, she only knows all the yellows and browns in Trivial Pursuit," he said, but he handed her the keys.

"Don't worry," Chelsea said, smiling up at him. She gave him a quick kiss.

As David strode down the dock away from his boat, the *Paramour*, a name chosen by the previous owner, he heard Chelsea say, "All right, guys. Sit down and we're going to go over the ground rules."

He smiled.

When he came up for air some five hours later there was a message from Chelsea. They'd had a ball, everyone was safe and sound and they were at his place. She would stay with the kids until he got home.

He arrived home at one o'clock in the morning, exhausted. He let himself in as quietly as possible. Chelsea wasn't in the living room. Despite his weariness, he felt himself smile. He forced himself to check on the kids first, saw that they were soundly sleeping, then went to his bedroom. Chelsea was sleeping in the middle of the bed, fully dressed, the comforter over her.

He had a strong feeling of well-being at the sight of her. He supposed it was a throwback to the male coming home to his waiting female. He wanted very much to make love to her, but frankly doubted he could manage it even if the kids weren't down the hall.

He stripped off his clothes and climbed in next to her. Just for a little while, he thought; then he'd move to the living room. She muttered something in her sleep when he cuddled against her bottom. He lightly kissed the back of her neck, still thinking that in just five minutes he'd leave.

He was asleep in two minutes.

And didn't wake up.

"Oh, my God! No, Mark, Taylor, go in the living room. Now!"

David forced an eye open to see Margaret, red faced, standing in the bedroom door, hands on hips, with the expression of a hanging judge.

"What are you doing here?" he asked, shaking his head to clear his brain.

"What is *she* doing here?" Out came a pointing finger. "In bed with you, and your children here!"

For a brief moment David didn't know what she was talking about, then he felt Chelsea beside him, stirring now, and froze. He cursed.

Chelsea came awake suddenly, with all her faculties alert, as was her habit. She was first aware of David, beautifully naked, lying beside her, then Margaret standing rigid in the doorway, in a Parent-Catching-Teenagers pose.

This is a farce and therefore funny, she told herself.

"Hello, Margaret," she said, pushing her hair off her forehead. She yawned. "Hello, David. When did you come home?"

He felt like a complete and utter fool. "Late," he said abruptly. He started to jump out of bed, realized he was naked, and said to Margaret, "I'll be out in a few minutes. Kindly remove yourself."

"We had a great time sailing, David," Chelsea said, her eyes on his body as he strode across the bedroom. "Of course, we missed you. David, I hesitate to mention this, but you don't have any clothes on."

"I know," he said, not facing her. He grabbed shorts and jeans, pulling them on as fast as he could.

She saw that he was upset and said reasonably, "David, I'm completely dressed. There is nothing to be perturbed over. Just because Margaret—that was Margaret, wasn't it?"

"Yes, and the bathroom is through there," he said. The rest of his words were muffled as he pulled a turtleneck over his head.

Chelsea frowned. She'd done nothing remotely questionable and neither had David. Why was he acting like this—guilty and angry? Angry at her! "Don't forget your deodorant," she said in the nastiest voice she could dredge up.

"Look, Chels," he said. "Oh, forget it. Stay put, it might be better. I'll handle this."

"There is no *this*," Chelsea called after him, but he paid no attention. "To handle," she ended on a mumble.

I'm supposed to stay in his bedroom like some sort of paid hooker? You're being redundant, turkey! Of course hookers are paid. Stop laughing at this situation, she told the small interior voice that persisted in seeing the entire morning as a farce.

She threw off the comforter and took herself to the bathroom. When she emerged with clean teeth, clean face and wrinkled clothes some ten minutes later, there were very civilized voices coming from the living room.

A masculine voice that wasn't David's. Aha, she thought, the general.

She strolled in. "Good morning."

"How dare you—" Margaret said in the calmest voice, but her teeth were gritted.

"That's enough!" David roared.

"I agree. Hello, sir. I'm Chelsea Lattimer."

A very straight, slender gentleman with crisp gray hair rose and took her hand. "My name is Nathan Monroe. A pleasure."

Chelsea heard Margaret begin to fuel up again and quickly said, "All right, I think this has gone on long enough. If you're not aware of it, Margaret, your children are standing in the kitchen, all ears. Your attitude is absurd, and I resent you giving David grief for sleeping in his own bed, despite whoever else might be in it. It would have served your nosiness right if we'd been doing all sorts of perverse, kinky things. As it was, if you'd bothered to open your eyes and close your mouth, you would have seen that I was fully dressed. Now I want my morning coffee. A pleasure to meet you, sir."

She made her exit, chin up, back straight.

Mark and Taylor stood like two rigid puppets in the middle of the kitchen. "Hi, guys," Chelsea said, making a straight line toward the coffeepot.

"Mother's angry," Mark said.

"She said you were a loose woman," Taylor said.

"The general told her to be quiet," Mark said.

"And I don't want to hear anymore until I've drunk half a cup. All right?"

Chelsea sat at the kitchen table and drank her coffee. Her mind was in high gear, and she was furious at Margaret for upsetting the children for no reason at all. After all, what had she been doing with the general, anyway? Playing gin rummy?

David came into the kitchen looking utterly distracted.

"Is it safe to come out yet?" Chelsea asked, a grin on her face.

"Is Mother still mad?" Mark asked.

"I'll take you home, Chels," David said wearily.

"Want to escape, huh?"

His eyes narrowed on her face. He was tired, angry at the absurd situation, and here was Chelsea being a pain in the butt along with Margaret.

"Yes, if you wish to be flippant about it."

Chelsea very carefully set down her coffee mug. "David," she said carefully, "I apologize for being flippant, but I simply can't take all this brouhaha seriously. You can't take me home, because if you do, you'll just have to take a taxi back. I drove the kids back here, remember?"

He felt even more like a fool than he had five minutes before.

Chelsea softened a bit. "Why is Margaret back early?"

"We met your parents in Honolulu, Chelsea," said the general from the kitchen door. "They send their love."

The light dawned very clearly. Chelsea threw back her head and laughed heartily. "Oh, dear, you poor man! You look all right. You survived?"

The general smiled, a nice smile, Chelsea noted. "Oh, yes." He gave David a commiserating look. "I'm sorry about this, Dr. Winter. Margaret insisted that we come. She's suffering from jet lag, I think. I'm going to take her back to the hotel now. I think you folks need some peace for a while. Please, Chelsea, don't leave. We will."

He added as he left the kitchen, "I think it would be nice if all of us went to dinner this evening. Can you get a sitter for the children?"

"Yes," Chelsea said. "I'll call George, David. She's bound to know of someone."

"But—" Mark said.

"You need to calm Mother down," Taylor said with appallingly candid insight to her father. "Chelsea's right. This is a brou-ha-ha."

The general laughed.

Chelsea grinned.

David sighed deeply.

The general said, "Incidentally, Chelsea, your folks flew back with us. They're staying at the Fairmont."

"Merciful heavens," Chelsea said.

"Oh, hell," David said.

"Dad!"

"Father!"

"I think I'll take up practice in Little America," David said.

"Where's that, Dad?" Mark said.

"The Antarctic. Trivial Pursuit, blue, geography."

Chelsea sat back in her chair and stretched out her legs in front of her. "Merciful heavens, David, I am impressed. I never would have gotten that one right."

"I looked through some of the questions before we started playing."

"Dad," Taylor said, "you look awful tired."

"I am. I think I'll go back to bed for a while."

"With Chelsea, Dad?" Mark said.

"Look, guys," David began, his brow furrowing, "would you all please just leave dear old Dad alone for a while?"

Chelsea laughed.

Chapter 13

I will forget this evening eventually, Chelsea thought, trying to concentrate on the delicious *sole meunière* and parsley potatoes. They were dining at the Carnelian Room high atop the Bank of America. The view was unbelievable, as usual, the service perfection itself, and the conversation, dominated by Margaret, was so civilized that Chelsea thought she would come down with lockjaw from gritting her teeth to keep silent. As for Mark's earlier comment that David needed to calm down Margaret, well, no one could be more calm than Margaret.

Chelsea didn't realize until the end of the meal that the general, bless his socks, had been steering Margaret skillfully into unexceptionable shoals, away from deep water. Then, unfortunately, the general excused himself for a moment. Chelsea looked after him wistfully, even as Margaret's voice, still civilized, but now with a layer of ice, said, "The children, you understand, Miss Lattimer, are terribly impressionable."

"And will continue to be so until they're eighteen, I imagine," Chelsea said. "Then they will magically know everything." She tossed a smile toward David. "Ah, that freshman year in college, the height of one's mental powers."

"Yes, well, it is important that they have the right *influences*, don't you agree?"

"I believe I see a roomful of probable good influences," Chelsea said.

"Perhaps," Margaret said, her cultured voice becoming a bit shrill. "It is simply different from what they're used to. David understands what I mean."

David arched a thick brow. "What I understand, Margaret, is that the world is full of people and children adapt marvelously well."

The general returned, but the spigot was open now, full blast, and Margaret continued without pause, her coffee cup jingling a bit. "I met the Lattimers, Chelsea's parents," she said, as if clinching the matter.

"Margaret," the general said in his calm deep voice, closing his hand over hers, "Harold and Mimi are delightful people."

"*He* wears gold chains and half *her* sentences are in high school French!"

"Oh, no," Chelsea said, laughing. "Mother never had high school French. She picked that up when she was in Paris. After she visits Vienna this summer it will be fractured German again. I have always found it most amusing. As for my father," Chelsea added, her voice losing a bit of its lightness, "he enjoys life, gold chains and all, and he doesn't hurt other people."

"They are very caring people, Margaret," David said. "I met them when Chelsea had to have emergency surgery."

This elicited an odd look from Margaret, who suddenly announced, "I believe I shall go to the ladies' room."

The general, an officer and a gentleman, rose to help her.

"Won't you come with me, Miss Lattimer?" Margaret asked from her new commanding height.

Chelsea winked at David. She leaned down and whispered in his ear as she passed his chair, "She's going to bring out the heavy guns now. This ought to be fun."

"Be serious, Chelsea," David said.

She looked at him for a long, steady moment. "I'd hoped we were beyond that," she said, and left.

David cursed softly into his coffee cup. A waiter hovered, and David waved him away. The general said in his deep, pleasant voice, "Chelsea is a charming young woman. Her parents are also charming. Margaret is charming when she doesn't feel threatened and manages to forget that she's a snob. She does forget it more and more now, David."

"Yes, of course, certainly. Did you enjoy Honolulu?" David asked, striving for a little charm himself. But he felt abused and a bit angry. Damn Chelsea, anyway! This was serious, and she was treating the entire situation as if it were an amusing part of one of her novels.

"Yes, certainly. It's difficult, I think, to change one's attitudes. To view life, if you will, from more than one angle. Incidentally, I am going to marry

Margaret. We will live in Washington. She will enjoy it.''

David's eyes fastened on the general's face. "The kids," he said, swallowing.

"I'm delighted that Margaret, despite her motives, left us alone for a while. Don't worry about Chelsea. That young woman can certainly handle Margaret at her most...well, in her Mrs. Full Charge mode. I have three grown children, David, and I find yours delightful. I am not their father—you are. I will convince Margaret that half their time should be spent with you.''

"Good luck," David said, now staring at the dregs in the bottom of his cup.

"No, I don't believe luck is involved." He paused a moment. "You never knew how to handle Margaret, or you were simply too busy with your medical studies, and then you didn't care, because both of you grew in different directions. I assume that you do want to see more of your children?''

"Certainly," he snapped, then sighed deeply. "Life is never simple or clear-cut, is it?''

"No, but that would be boring," said the general. "You should have been in World War II. We would have won much sooner, I suspect.''

The general laughed.

"What a lovely shade of lipstick," Chelsea was saying to Margaret at that moment. She'd spent an unconscionable amount of time in the stall, not to annoy Margaret, but to get herself under control. Damn David, anyway! Reverting to being a stuffed shirt again, without a bit of humor!

Margaret said nothing, merely continued outlining her mouth with a shade Chelsea had to admire.

Chelsea sat in a stool beside her and gazed into the mirror. "Oh, dear, my hair always informs me when it's damp outside." She began pulling a comb through her bouncing curls.

Margaret said abruptly, "I know you're sleeping with David."

"It's all a wager," Chelsea said. "A scientific study, as it were. Since you arrived, however, our lab work has been severely curtailed. Actually," she added with a mournful voice, "it's been nonexistent." She heard David's voice telling her to be serious. Dratted man, she was serious when it was warranted, wasn't she?

"I assume you enjoy sleeping with him."

There was no cattiness in Margaret's voice, and Chelsea frowned. Perhaps, she thought, she should be just a bit less flighty and flippant. "Yes," she said, her voice softening involuntarily as she met Margaret's eyes in the mirror. "Yes, I do. He is a very sexy man and a very nice man."

"David, unlike most men," Margaret said after a brief pause, "doesn't sleep around. He did not leave me for another woman. To the best of my knowledge he was faithful to me until the divorce. He left me because we no longer cared about our life together."

"I don't think I'll ever marry," Chelsea said. She added quickly, "Not that I'm criticizing, by any means. Commitments are tough, and I, for one, don't think I care to try one so binding as marriage."

Margaret gave her a funny look, then fished in her makeup bag for her compact. "I am worried about my children," she said after a long pause. "It's not that I don't believe what you just said. It's just that if David decides he wants you, he will win, don't doubt it.

He's very forceful. Do you know this is the first time that he's spent so much time with his children?''

"I suspected that."

"During the last two years of our marriage he spent more and more time at the hospital—to avoid me, of course. Unfortunately, it also meant not seeing his children."

"That must have been difficult," Chelsea said.

"David has changed," Margaret said, frowning a bit. "The children don't realize it, of course. They tell me that Father said this and that, and I stare at them. Perhaps it's the California air, or more likely it's knowing someone like you." Margaret turned and faced Chelsea straightly. "I've been something of a bitch to you, and I apologize. The children like you very much."

"I like them," Chelsea said. "I will try to loosen them up, Margaret, if I spend time with them. But I don't believe that involves corrupting their young minds."

"No, I guess not. Taylor showed me what she called her Marin sailing togs. Those pink sneakers are too much."

"Taylor is already showing signs of being a good sailor. Mark, too, for that matter."

"I'm pleased about that. I do want my children to enjoy themselves. May I call you 'Chelsea'?" At Chelsea's pleased nod Margaret continued, saying unexpectedly, "David told me the kind of novels you wrote, and I shuddered and made disapproving noises, which, of course, he expected me to. Actually, I enjoy reading long historicals, and I've read several of yours. They take one to a different time, away from all the complexities of the modern age, and make one, well, feel that there can be an ideal relationship between a man and a woman. Am I making any sense at all?"

"Oh, goodness, yes," Chelsea said. She added thoughtfully, "You know something, Margaret? I think I've been wearing blinders. I spouted off once to David that women didn't want to read about men like their husbands—you know, beer bellies and all that—but that isn't true at all. Maybe that's true sometimes, but I think it's just as you said. Romance is a hard quality to maintain when you're surrounded by the daily demands of work and family and fixing leaky faucets. Perhaps reading a novel, or seeing a romantic movie simply brings romance to the fore again and improves things. Ah, tell me to shut up." Chelsea grinned. "Once I get going, it's like the Rough Riders going full charge up that hill."

"Not at all. I've never met an author before. Perhaps, between us, we've made the definitive statement."

"Sounds reasonable to me."

"You really didn't make love to David last night, did you?"

Chelsea laughed. "I slept like a log. Poor man, he probably didn't get home until very late and was dead on his feet. There'd been a major emergency, a wreck on 101. It was on the news." Her voice became very sober, and as serious as David could have wished. "Margaret, I had told him that I would stay with the kids until he got back from the hospital. I did, and I eventually went to sleep. I would not have made loud and passionate love with your children down the hall."

Margaret laughed. She rose and smoothed down her dark blue silk dress. "You know something?"

Chelsea cocked her head.

"I think I shall make loud and passionate love tonight."

"Go for it," Chelsea said.

"Bizarre," David said. "I felt like I'd been put through an experience warp."

Margaret, the general and the kids had gone to the zoo, and David and Chelsea were at a hamburger joint, south of Market Street nearly shouting to be heard over the din.

"I had the same feeling. You know something else, David? I think everything is going to work out for you. And for Mark and Taylor. And for Margaret and the general."

David took a big bite out of his hamburger, chewed thoughtfully, then said, "I had consigned the evening to perdition when Margaret started on you."

"Well, we've still got this evening to go. Mom and Dad, you know. Drinks at the Hyatt."

David, diverted, said, "If they like the Hyatt so much, why don't they stay there? It's quite a taxi ride from the Fairmont to the Embarcadero."

Chelsea said primly, her eyes sparkling, "The Hyatt is too *moderne*. *Très chic*, *naturellement*, *mais trop*— Gallic shrug—*je ne sais pas quoi*. Another Gallic shrug."

"This is terrible. I understood you!" He sat forward suddenly and clasped her hands between his. "You're a brick, Chels."

Chelsea ran her tongue over her lower lip. "Do bricks get horny, David? Like turnips?"

His hands tightened on hers. "When do we have to see your parents?"

"Not for another three hours," she said, trying for a seductive look. She succeeded, and David sucked in his breath.

They arrived at David's flat twenty minutes later, and three minutes later than that they were in the bedroom, their clothing in a straight line from the entrance hall.

"David," she gasped as he tossed her onto her back and pulled her legs over his shoulders, "this isn't at all scientific!"

He lowered his head and began to caress her and love her. "David, I—" She had no idea what she would have said, for at that moment she felt her body go haywire. She tugged at his hair, gasping at the intense sensations washing through her. "I don't believe this," she moaned; then her body arched upward as he thrust deeply into her. She felt him moving in her, felt his fingers find her, and she was gone.

But David held back. He didn't know how he did it, but he did. He brought her to pleasure two more times, reveling in the look of utter astonishment on her face. Reveling in the feel of her, the intense heat of her body. He arched his back and exploded deep inside her, and she thought him the most beautiful sight in the universe—his neck muscles corded, his arms flexing, his eyes closed tightly.

"Is there still life in this male body?" she said after long moments of regaining breath and voice.

"No, not even an ounce." David raised himself a bit so he could see her face. "Chelsea," he said, his voice uncertain, even wary, "I've never felt anything like that before."

"You're complaining?"

"No, it scares me." He stopped and blinked, and she wondered what he would have said. He grinned now. "Do you know how great you just were, lady?"

She flushed, and David laughed. "I finally got you, huh? It's about time. I watched you and felt you—three times. It was great."

"I've never done that before," she said in a surprisingly shy voice. "I thought it was only in novels, like mine."

"So you think we're ready to publish the results of our study? Woman Succumbs to Superlover? Woman Gives All? Woman Admits Existence of Passion?"

"All right, all right, you win," Chelsea said. "But you know, David, it could simply have been the result of...deprivation!"

"Do you still feel deprived?"

"No, not at all. I feel on the brink of terminal satiation."

"You writers—what kind of a word is that?"

She was trying to find another retort, when he began kissing her. She felt his smooth, deft fingers glide over her breasts, pausing to gently fondle her nipples. To her utter shock, her body responded.

And responded.

"Some satiation," he murmured against her breast.

Shadows were lengthening, casting the bedroom into dimness.

"Oh, my God!" Chelsea nearly shouted. "We've got to meet my parents in thirty minutes!"

They were late, of course. David whispered in her ear as they entered the hotel, "They're going to know what we've been doing. Your eyes look so soft they'd melt a knife."

"Mac the knife or David the knife?"

"Cookie!" Harold Lattimer embraced his daughter, eyed her for a long moment and said, "So that's why you're late. Mimi, you need to speak to this daughter of yours!"

Chelsea groaned, and David had the grace to look a bit embarrassed.

"*Bonjour*, David," said Mimi, kissing him on his cheek. "Do sit down and tell us about Chelsea's scar. *Entre nous*, of course!"

"Mother?"

"Cookie, you're sounding like a prude, and life is too short for that. What do you want to drink? More of that wimpy white wine? Waiter!"

David sat back and watched the wildly volleying jokes. When it was his turn, which it was very quickly, he said seriously, "The scar is only about four inches long, she can still wear a bikini and the scar tissue is minimal. I scarcely notice it."

"David!"

"Now, Cookie, don't be so serious." Harold Lattimer beamed at David and said, "When are you two getting hitched? Mind you, David, I didn't think my little girl would ever find a man to suit her, but it appears that you're suiting her just fine. What do you think, Mimi?"

"It sounds as if he is keeping a close eye on her scar, *je crois*," said Mimi.

Chelsea choked on her white wine. "Never, never again," she declared, "will you guys go to Hawaii. You've become outrageous and decadent! You're embarrassing David. Now let's talk about your vacation. Censored, of course." There was a brief pause, a knowing look between her parents, and Chelsea said,

"Just look at those elevators. It's like Buck Rogers in the twenty-fifth century, isn't it—"

"Chelsea," David said, taking her hand. "Shut up."

"Merciful heavens," Harold said after a long moment. "She did. What do you think about that, Mimi?"

"I hope, *j'espère*, that she isn't pregnant before the wedding."

David choked on his scotch. He hadn't used anything, nor had Chelsea. He felt an awful sense of fate descending on his head. Then he felt something he'd never felt before: a sense of well-being, a sense of rightness. He shot Chelsea a look, but she was looking frantic and nearly shouting, "Waiter! I want another glass of white wine!"

"Mon Dieu," said Mimi. "Another margarita!"

"I feel battered, bruised, bent and otherwise mutilated," Chelsea said, slouching in the passenger seat of David's car.

"I didn't use anything, Chelsea," David said, studiously watching traffic before he pulled out of their parking spot.

"Join the club," Chelsea said. And she started praying in Latin.

"Chelsea, could we have—"

"David, please. I don't know. I'm very erratic, oh, forget it!"

She slouched even farther down, her knees against the dash. "Please forget what my parents said—they were off the wall. Marriage is ridiculous. Out of the question."

David finally got himself into the heavy traffic on Market Street. He said blandly, not looking at her, "Lots of people do it."

"Yeah, and lots of people don't make it."

"Yes, true enough." He thought glumly that she'd just experienced first-secondhand what a divorce was like. Well, it wasn't that bad. But he saw that she was scared, skittish, and he didn't know what to say. What if he *had* gotten her pregnant? He swallowed. He decided, his scientific persona coming to the fore, that he would monitor the situation closely in the upcoming weeks.

Why not get married? He rather hoped suddenly that he had gotten her pregnant.

No, that wasn't fair. Nothing seemed particularly fair at the moment, or particularly clear. He felt a surge of desire for her, followed by a spurt of impatience. For heaven's sake, she wasn't exactly *young*. One would think that he was something of a good catch, wouldn't one? He wasn't fat, he wasn't bald, he was a good lover, damn it. What woman wouldn't want him?

Stupid sod.

Chapter 14

David paused a moment at his front door, momentarily nonplussed. Raucous laughter, squeals and general hilarity were coming from inside.

When he strolled into his living room he saw Chelsea, Mark and Taylor all sitting on the floor in front of a blazing fire, playing, of all things, chess.

Chelsea was saying, "Now, Mark, the rook doesn't go in a diagonal, the bishop does. Look!"

"Check, Chelsea!" Taylor shouted.

"All right, you guys, this isn't fair! We put your ages together and you still don't come near to me, and therefore you can't beat me. Aha! See, my knight goes here in front of my poor king."

"He's pinned!" Mark announced with great glee.

"You got that right, kiddo," Chelsea said. "What are you going to do about it? I'm awfully devious, so be careful."

"Dad!" Taylor jumped to her feet and then ran into his arms.

David wrapped his arms around his daughter and squeezed. "What is going on here?" he asked over Taylor's head.

Mark took his turn to be hugged by his father. "We're tromping Chelsea, Dad."

"If you know what a pin is you obviously are," David said, smiling at Chelsea over his son's head.

Both kids were wearing jeans and baggy shirts. All three *kids* were barefoot.

It was at that precise moment that David made up his mind to marry Chelsea Lattimer. He didn't question his decision. He just let it flow through him, making him feel pleasantly warm, making his world expand by two continents.

"Come on, Dad, Chelsea needs help—bad!"

"Hi, dear old Dad," Chelsea said, rising. She hugged him, resting her cheek against his shoulder for a moment.

"You still alive with these little devils?"

"We're fine. You look tired. You okay?"

He tightened his arms around her, leaned down and whispered in her ear, "I'm just fine, but I am feeling a bit . . . deprived."

"Dad, you're kissing Chelsea again!"

"At least," Mark said to his sister, disgust in his young voice, "he's not touching her bottom."

"Yeck," Taylor said.

"Just wait until she's eleven or twelve," Chelsea said. "Yeck will turn to wow."

"Boys are stupid," Taylor said.

"What about silly girls?" Mark began, and David groaned.

"I'm going to get a beer. How about you, Chels?"

"A beer, Dad?" Taylor's eyes widened. "You never used to drink that stuff."

"It's the working man's drink, and I am a working man," David said.

"White wine for me," Chelsea said. "That, you guys, is the working woman's drink."

The kids were so wound up that it wasn't until eleven o'clock that they were finally tucked into bed. David dropped onto the sofa beside Chelsea. "Lord, what an evening."

"Lots of fun," Chelsea said. "I'll give you chess lessons, too, David," she added provocatively.

"Let's neck, instead," he said, and pulled her onto his lap.

David saw movement from the corner of his eye and said without turning his head, "Get back to bed or I'm going to turn into a monster. It's my turn to have Chelsea's attention. Scoot!"

"Yes, Dad."

"Yes, Father."

David leaned his head back against the sofa pillows. "They've certainly changed," he said.

Chelsea stiffened just a bit. "What do you mean?"

"They're ... children, I guess, not little regimented soldiers."

"Don't let the general hear you say that." She wrapped her arms around his neck and nestled closer. "I missed you."

"Me, too," he said, his eyes closed, his entire body relaxed. It occurred to him suddenly that Chelsea had acted like a glorified baby-sitter for him. "Chels," he began, his hand rubbing up and down her back, "I appreciate all the time you've spent with the kids."

"My pleasure," she said. "I've never been around children before. It's been fun. Truly."

"I just don't want you to think that I've, well, that I've been using you."

"I think there probably are things you could feel guilty about, Dr. Winter, but the kids aren't one of them." She added thoughtfully, after nibbling at his earlobe, "I've learned a lot from them. And something else neat—they're already very socialized, but they still blurt out what they're thinking, and it usually knocks my socks off."

"I don't think they used to blurt out anything," David said.

Chelsea squirmed a bit to get more comfortable, and David groaned. "I'm in bad shape," he said.

"Unfortunately there's nothing to be done about it, Dr. Winter."

"Then hold your bottom still, or I'll fling you on the floor and ravish you."

She laughed and pressed her breasts against him. "I need to get myself home and get some sleep. I promised Mark and Taylor that I'd help them pack all their San Francisco goodies. What time is their flight to Washington?"

"Just before noon. Thank God they like the general. Mark's all excited about visiting the space museum, or whatever it's called."

Chelsea realized that she would miss them and asked very carefully, "When will they be coming out here again?"

"In April, for a week. Then I'll have them for about six weeks this summer."

"That's not too long to wait," she said, squirmed a bit, then jumped to her feet. "Now where did I put my sneakers?"

He hadn't meant to do it, but the words just came out without his permission. In the middle of the San Francisco airport. With hundreds of people nearby. They'd just deposited the kids with Margaret and the general, said their goodbyes and waved again as Mark and Taylor disappeared down the corridor to the plane.

Chelsea stared at him. "What did you say, David?"

He looked away from her, wishing he could retract the words, to save them for an intimate moment, but it was too late. He said, his teeth gritted, "I said that I want you to marry me, Chelsea."

"That's what I thought you said," she said, and kept walking toward the escalator.

David looked at her back and got angry. He caught up with her in a moment and grabbed her arm. "What the hell kind of an answer is that?"

"That, David," Chelsea said, "wasn't an answer. It was just a bunch of words that didn't mean anything to fill in time while I tried to figure out why you asked me what you did in the first place."

"I didn't mean it . . . that is, I didn't mean to do it here, just after we saw the kids off with Margaret and the general . . . in the most unromantic place—"

"I understand," said Chelsea, who didn't understand at all. "Please, David, let's wait. Really, I don't think—"

It was his turn to cut her off. "I would have expected you to say something a bit more . . . loving."

A harried businessman bumped her with his clothes bag, apologized and rushed on.

Chelsea felt as though the world had tilted and she was going to fall off. Marriage! He couldn't mean it, not really. It had been brought on by the fact that she got along so well with his children. He saw her as their surrogate mother, saw them all together in a blissful, utterly fictionalized future, where all was sweetness and light and good fun. David was merely confused.

She said, "Let's go have a toothsome Mexican dinner."

"What?"

"I'm hungry, and I want my dinner."

He clamped down on what he'd intended to say. He'd give her two glasses of white wine, then trot out his good qualities for her inspection and obvious approval.

He managed a smile and said, "Onward. To Mill Valley? The Cantina?"

"Yes," said Chelsea, not looking at him.

The Cantina was crowded, and they had to wait twenty minutes for a table. David made certain she drank two glasses of wine during that time. He spoke only of things at the hospital, to which she responded with an appropriate positive or negative. He wished he knew what she was thinking.

He ordered a third glass of white wine for her over her taco salad. She raised an eyebrow at him, but said nothing. David didn't drink a thing.

"Chelsea," he began, "about what I said at the airport—"

"I will think about what you said, David, if you're certain you still feel the same."

"I still feel the same. I want to marry you."

"I will think—"

"Damn it! Just listen to me a minute. Chelsea, I'm not a pauper. My income is reasonable. I can support you—" He swallowed on that faux pas and shook his head. "What I meant to say is that I'm not a pauper. You enjoy making love with me. We have fun together." He stopped, thinking it ridiculous that he should have to be selling himself to her. She either knew all that already or she didn't. She either wanted to marry him or she didn't. He said nothing more, merely speared a bite of his enchilada and chewed.

"You're from Boston," Chelsea said, not looking up from her meal.

"That certainly is a profound statement," he said.

"What I mean is that I...well, I want to think about it, David. Please, give me some time."

And that was that, he thought. She gave him a rather curious, puzzled look when he walked her to her front door, but didn't invite him in, just sent him on his way at ten o'clock at night. It didn't occur to him until much later that he hadn't told her that he loved her. He smacked his palm against his forehead. Dumb!

It was Elsa who told him that a lady wanted to speak to him on the phone. David, in the middle of stitching up a six-year-old's head, grunted and asked Elsa to take a message. Elsa hadn't told him it was Chelsea Lattimer.

It was close to six o'clock in the evening when he finally broke free. When he saw Chelsea's name on the message slip he frowned and quickly dialed her number. Three rings, and then her damned answering machine.

"If this is David," a subdued voice said, "the answer is no. I'm sorry. This is, ah, Chelsea."

David stared at the phone as if it were something alien and quite distasteful. He heard the buzz. Damn it, she hadn't even said enough to fill up the free time between buzzes.

He rang her up every thirty minutes until midnight. Same message. By the time he dragged himself to bed his silent fury with her had changed to outraged anger. He cursed her until he fell asleep.

The next morning he called again. Her regular message was on the machine, not the special one she'd left for him. He cursed her through his shower, breakfast and drive to the hospital.

By afternoon he was back to silent fury.

By evening he wanted to cry in his beer.

"Chels, where the devil are you?"

"Up at the Heritage House in Mendocino," Chelsea said to George. "Look, George, I just wanted to get away for a while."

George looked thoughtfully out the window, then back to the phone. "It's been nearly a week. Have you been there all that time?"

"Yes."

"You really didn't have to run away, Chelsea."

Chelsea chewed on her lower lip. "Is David all right?"

"If you mean by that is he still acting like a human being, the answer is mostly. He finally fessed up to Elliot yesterday. I think he'd like to beat you silly, Chels. You really didn't explain anything to him, did you?"

There was a deep sigh on the line. "No, not really, I guess."

"Do you love him?"

"Well, yes. No. I'm not really certain, George. How 'bout I'm miserable and leave it at that?"

George was silent for a moment, then said crisply, "I think I'll drive up to see you today. How does that sound?"

"Just promise not to tell David, all right?"

"You got it."

At two o'clock that afternoon George found Chelsea in the beautiful restored Victorian sitting room-bar at the Heritage House. She looks awful, George thought, staring at her friend before Chelsea was aware of her presence. There were shadows beneath her eyes, testifying to sleepless nights, and her fingers were nervously plucking at her slacks. What a mess, George thought, planted a smile on her face and strode forward.

"Hi," Chelsea said.

"Hi, yourself," George said, then sat down on the old sofa beside her friend. "You look like a reject from—"

"Don't say it. Too true. A silly, weak woman is always supposed to look like this. George, I blew it!"

George saw the tears swimming in her friend's eyes and quickly rose. "Let's go for a walk along the cliffs."

A stiff breeze was blowing up from the ocean, but the sun was bright overhead. "It's so beautiful here," George said, taking a deep breath. "When I was last here with Elliot, I didn't get to see much of the scenery. Thank heavens the cottages are interesting in themselves."

Chelsea didn't say anything, merely leaned down, picked up a pebble and flung it with precision out into the water.

"You want to tell me about it, Chels?"

"He asked me to marry him at the airport. I was so taken aback that I didn't say one sensible thing. Then at dinner he started telling me all about his... prospects, I guess the word is."

To Chelsea's surprise and disgruntlement, George laughed. "I'm sorry, Chels, but I did the exact same thing to Elliot, only we were thirty-five thousand feet in the air. I told him all about my investments, how I'd pull my own weight and all that stuff. He looked at me as if I'd lost my marbles."

"What happened?"

"He put me off, just as you did David. Eventually he told me no. He'd prepared this damned speech, all about my growing career and his ancient years and how it couldn't work. I wanted to kill him, as I recall."

"You never told me that," Chelsea said.

"Well, I'm telling you now. Actually, I didn't tell anybody. It hurt too much at the time."

"Does David hurt, do you think?"

"For heaven's sake, Chels, he asked you to marry him, didn't he?" George gave her a fond, exasperated look. "Of course he loves you. How can you doubt that?"

"He didn't say anything about love."

"Goodness, you must really have had him going!"

"George, look, I think he asked me to marry him because we'd had such fun with his kids, and he saw me as being the perfect surrogate mother for them.

You know, all sweetness and light. At least, that's what I thought.''

"I never realized David was such a shallow person," George said. "But, then again, I suppose you know him best."

"Shallow! He isn't shallow!"

"But, Chelsea," George said reasonably, "you just said that he didn't love you, he just wanted a glorified baby-sitter."

"George, why don't you just leave and smile up at me from a cover on a magazine!"

"Can't take the heat, huh, Chels? All right, I'll stop ragging you. Now you can't stay up here for the rest of your life. What do you intend to do?''

"Go home and see him, I guess," Chelsea said, her voice more resigned than glum.

"And what will you tell him?"

Chelsea stopped, sat down on an outcropping of rock and dangled her legs. She said after a moment, "George, will you please stop pacing in front of me? You look so bloody beautiful, it makes me feel like a toad."

Obligingly George sat down beside her. "Now we're two toads sunning ourselves on a warm rock. Talk, toad."

Three minutes of dead silence followed.

"I know you've been spending hours thinking, Chels. Why don't you just think out loud?"

"Oh, all right. David is from Boston."

"Good grief, a capital offense!"

"That's not exactly what I mean. I mean that he and I couldn't be more different. He's got to think I'm a flake, George, even though he's probably forced himself not to believe it right now. You know, a good-time girl who's never serious. A person who makes his kids face up to being kids and not little stuffed shirts. And he's still got to be a stuffed shirt. People don't really change, George, you know that, even though his ex-wife told me he had. He'd be at me within six months to stop joking around and running off at the mouth.''

"Hmmmm."

"And he said nothing at all about loving me. I think he's lonely and sex starved, that's all."

"And you make him laugh, right?"

"Yeah."

"And you enjoy each other in bed, right?"

"Yeah. He won that wager. I kept thinking that the next time we'd make love I'd yawn and want to read."

"Hmmmm."

"It just kept getting better," Chelsea added in a mournful voice.

"That certainly sounds suspicious. I agree with you, Chels. I'm so bored with Elliot now that I've read everything on the bestseller list just to keep myself going."

"You are not! Elliot can't keep his hands off you, and you're always draped all over him!"

George arched a perfect eyebrow. "Really?" she said in a drawling voice.

"You're a rat, George, or a rattess."

"And you, Chelsea Lattimer, are an idiot. Do you love David?"

"Damn it, yes, but I'm not going to marry him. George, just imagine all the problems we'd have. It just wouldn't work."

"What problems?"

"Well," Chelsea said finally, "lots of problems. I just can't think of any right now. He'd turn back into a stuffed shirt within six months."

"Actually, I only see David as a stuffed shirt when he turns seventy."

"Maybe, maybe not. I just wish he didn't look and act like one of my heroes most of the time."

George fell silent, and Chelsea didn't see the wicked gleam in her eyes. She said, "I wonder what a hero would do with you, the heroine?"

"Something outrageous, doubtless. David isn't ever outrageous. He's too dignified."

"Even in bed?"

"Well, not usually. Well, never, actually."

"Hmmm."

"I guess what it boils down to, George, is that I'm just scared. Marriage is something that makes me start shaking. It's the heaviest commitment a person can make. What if I blow it?"

"Why would you blow it?"

"Well, just look at David and Margaret. They didn't make it, and they appear to have had everything in common. David and I are as different as . . . I can't think of anything original, and I don't want to be trite. Writers don't want to say the expected thing."

"Can you imagine two people any more different than Elliot and me? A doctor and a model? Lord, Chelsea, it's the differences that make life interesting. I carry on passionately about something, Elliot laughs, and we each end up seeing the other's point."

Chelsea was wearing her mulish look, George saw. "So what are you going to do?"

"I'm going home, and if he wants to hear it, I'll tell him that I want more time. Like a year or six. I don't want to be scared when we get married."

"That sounds like a plan," George said.

"What do you mean by that snide remark?"

"Snide? *Moi?* Chelsea, you're beginning to lose your sense of humor. Come on, let's go home." I've got things to do and miles to go before I sleep, she added silently.

And George, who looked angelic and didn't believe that people should stick their oars in, was prepared to launch a boat. She smiled lovingly and with great understanding at Chelsea, helped her check out of the Heritage House and followed her back to San Francisco.

Chapter 15

Elliot tried his most nonchalant voice. "So, David, what did Chelsea have to say?"

David shook himself like a mongrel dog and sat down beside Elliot at the poolside. "She said she wanted time to think about it, dithered around and hung up."

"Sounds reasonable, I suppose," Elliot said.

David cursed, drawing a disapproving glance from an older woman whose bulk should have prohibited the wearing of her bilious green swimsuit.

"Actually," David continued, "I felt like flinging her over my shoulder and carting her off someplace."

"As a matter of fact, perhaps that's the way to go," Elliot said, so relieved that David himself had gotten with George's program that every tense muscle in his body relaxed.

But David was on a roll and didn't hear him. "She's being so stubborn, so damned obtuse. She won't even let me see her, much less make love to her." He cursed again the moment the disapproving woman had moved away.

"I've got a plan," Elliot said.

David arched a thick dark brow. "Yes?"

"Well, actually, it's more George's plan than mine, all based on the fact that Chelsea loves you."

David looked inordinately pleased at that. "She told George that? That she loved me? You promise, Elliot, she really said that?"

"Yes, indeed. I also gather that she's convinced that you guys are going to continue to be dynamite in bed. She's just scared because, according to her, the two of you are so different. She's afraid that you're going to turn back into the stuffed shirt Mr. Hyde after six months."

David looked honestly surprised. "That's the stupidest thing I've ever heard!"

"Yes, I agree, but she's quite serious about it. That and wanting more time. I think she's also worried about making a commitment of such magnitude." Elliot stretched a bit, then said in an offhand voice, "As I said, George has a plan. As far as I can tell, it's foolproof."

"Tell me. Lord knows I'm ready to try anything."

"There's a poker game at Chelsea's house this Friday with the boys."

"I wasn't invited," David said.

"You'll be having lunch with Delbert, Angelo and Maurice on Union Street tomorrow."

"Why? Not that I don't like the *boys*, but what's the purpose? Do they want to borrow money?"

"No money involved. The *boys* are behind you one hundred percent. You'll work out the details of the plan with them tomorrow."

"It's not illegal, is it?"

"Oh, no," Elliot said as he slipped back into the water. "As a matter of fact, you're going to become a Mark I hero. Now, supermacho stud, how about a ten-lap race?"

"You ain't got a prayer!"

"What's the matter, Sweet Lips?" Delbert asked as he hugged Chelsea.

"Nothing," Chelsea said. "Why do you think anything's the matter?"

"You look like an onion whose skin has been peeled away."

"That's disgusting! Angelo, come take this fool away. You, Maurice, come help me with the goodies in the kitchen."

"What did perfect Sarah come up with this time?" Maurice asked, following her out of the room.

"She certainly appears to have it bad," Angelo said to Delbert. "We *are* doing the right thing."

"I hope so," Delbert said, scratching his head. "David better work everything out."

"Yeah, if he doesn't, there'll be no more poker games with Chelsea." This brought forth a worried look and a doleful sigh from the both of them.

It was nine o'clock, and Chelsea had lost nearly fifty dollars. She didn't care. She was still working on her first glass of white wine. When the doorbell rang she sloshed her glass onto the poker table.

"Go answer it, honey," Delbert told her. The moment she left the living room he poured her another glass of white wine and sprinkled a bit of white powder into it. He stirred it with his finger. "No turning back now," he said.

"She's miserable for sure," Angelo said. "Have you ever seen her lose so much money so soon?"

"And not give a damn," added Delbert.

"David!"

"Good to see you, old man!"

"Come sit down. I'll get you a beer."

Chelsea looked shell-shocked. She'd answered the door and seen him standing there, gorgeous, smiling and sexy. She'd backed up. Now, with her three friends behind her, she said, "What are you doing here? You weren't invited."

"Delbert asked me," David said with his most engaging smile. "Said he was broke and needed to win, thus my invitation. You don't mind, do you?"

"He's already won a great deal off me," Chelsea said. She felt wrung out and wanted to belt David and kiss his face at the same time. Instead she bumped into the table and her wineglass tipped over. She stared stupidly at the wine spreading over the cards and poker chips.

The four men stared at the empty glass, then shot comic looks at each other.

Angelo said, "Chels, honey, go get a dishcloth or something. I'll pour you another glass."

"Keep her in the kitchen for a bit," Angelo said, motioning to Delbert.

"No plan is perfect," Maurice said easily as he poured another glass of white wine and added his white powder. "You can use *your* finger to stir it this time, Doc."

For a long moment David didn't move. What he was doing was dishonest, ruthless, unfair, outrageous . . . *Mark I.* He stirred the wine with his finger.

He raised her glass out of the way while she and Delbert cleaned up the mess.

"Well," Chelsea said to David, "I suppose that since you're here you might as well play." She stomped out of the room and returned with another chair. "Sit and lose."

Chelsea was too miserable to realize that every sip of her wine was to the accompaniment of four interested pairs of eyes. She gambled wildly, and won. "You guys aren't paying attention," she said finally.

"Oh, yes, we are," Maurice said. "You just got lucky, Sweet Lips."

Chelsea won the next hand with a pair of threes, and she giggled. "I must be drinking too much," she remarked to her newly filled glass of wine. "I think I'll switch to soda water."

Everything was so funny. She no longer felt nervous with David sitting next to her at the table. She thought he was the finest thing she'd ever seen, and said so.

"Finest thing?" David said, grinning at her.

"Yes," Chelsea said, and tried to focus on his face. "And you've got the most beautiful teeth."

"Very white," Delbert agreed.

"I like it when you smile like that," Chelsea said, ignoring Delbert.

"I promise to smile like this for the next fifty years," David said. He gently covered her hand with his.

Chelsea stared down at his hand. "I feel odd," she said. David caught her as she fell forward.

"Step two coming up," said Angelo.

"Stay with her while I pack her bag," David said, and took himself to her bedroom.

Ten minutes later, after congratulations and at least a half-dozen rounds of good luck, David eased Chelsea into the passenger seat, fastened her seat belt and sped out of Sausalito.

Thirty minutes later he carried her on board a small charter plane.

"Too much to drink," he told the pilot.

"She's a little thing," the pilot observed. "You'll make sure she's well strapped in?"

"You got it," David said.

Just before they landed in Las Vegas, David slipped the gold band on her finger.

He kept humming under his breath, "I'm a Mark I hero, yours all the way... I'm a Mark I hero, here to stay...."

The motel was easy. David simply left her in the car and signed the register as Dr. and Mrs. David Winter.

He gazed at her hungrily after he'd taken off her clothes.

"You've lost weight," he told her, and she grunted softly in her sleep and rolled over. "Your bottom is still the greatest-looking behind I've ever seen."

It was nearly two o'clock in the morning when he slipped into bed beside her, curving spoon-fashion against her back.

He thought he'd go out of his mind with her beautifully naked beside him, but instead he fell asleep very quickly—the sleep of the ruthless, he thought.

Chelsea turned in her sleep and flowed into a large, very warm male body. It was nice, and she wrapped her arms around the warm, hairy chest.

She came awake on a sneeze. She opened her eyes slowly, saw that a tuft of hair was responsible for the tickling nose, blinked like an owl and squeaked.

David closed his arms around her and pulled her closer.

"David!"

The sound of her own voice sent shards of hangover through her head. David opened his eyes, looked up into her shocked face and smiled. "Good morning, love," he said.

Chelsea's mouth felt as if it were stuffed with damp cotton. "I don't feel well," she gasped. "This is a miserable nightmare.... I need some aspirin."

She pulled away from him, and he let her go. She managed to stand beside the bed, saw that she was naked, and gasped.

"Aspirin in the bathroom," David said.

She stumbled into the small bathroom, found the aspirin bottle beside her toothpaste and popped three of them down. She looked at her face, groaned at the dreadful apparition staring back at her and brushed her teeth. For want of anything better she wrapped a towel around herself and staggered back into the bedroom.

"I don't understand," she managed, staring at David, who was now sitting up in bed, the covers coming only to his middle.

"Come back to bed, Chels," he said in a very loving voice. "You'll feel better in no time at all, I promise." He was telling the truth. It wasn't aspirin in the

bottle, it was something stronger, designed to relieve
any ache, pain or hangover in the animal world.

"All right," she said. She slipped in beside him,
lying on her back, the towel still firmly around her. "I
don't understand," she said again. "Where are we?
What are you doing here?"

Now it begins, David thought. He turned on his side
toward her, balancing himself on his elbow. "We're in
Las Vegas," he said.

"Las Vegas! But..." She looked desperate. "We
were at my house! Where are Delbert and—"

"They're home, of course. They did see us off,
however. They send their congratulations." He allowed a few moments to show her his disappointment. "Don't you remember, Chels?"

She grew very still. The pain in her head was only a
dull throbbing now, and her brain and mouth felt as
if they were working in concert again. "I didn't have
any clothes on," she said. She turned to look at him.
"You don't have any clothes on, either."

"No, love. It was great between us. Don't you
agree?"

"We...we made love?"

"Chelsea," he said, trying to sound hurt, "did you
drink all that much?"

"No! That is, I remember the white wine and
then..." Her voice trailed off, and she pressed her
palms against the sides of her head.

"Chelsea, are you serious? You really don't remember what we did?"

She shook her head.

"You insisted that we get married right away. Nevada seemed like the best place. I managed to buy you
that wedding band."

Slowly, as if her hand belonged to someone else, Chelsea lowered it and stared at the simple gold band. She started shaking her head. "No, it can't be true...."

She sounded so bewildered and so frightened that he was ready to confess everything. He opened his mouth, but she forestalled him.

"I asked you to marry me?"

He made a noncommittal gesture that she took for an affirmative.

"And you did? Here in Las Vegas?"

"You don't remember the preacher?" he asked, unwilling to lie directly anymore.

She shook her head, looking even more miserable.

I'm simply not a Mark I hero who's ruthless and outrageous, he decided, and said, "Chelsea—"

Chelsea turned toward him at that moment and pressed herself against him. She rested her cheek against his shoulder. He stared down at her tousled head and very tentatively closed his arms around her back.

"I remember now," Chelsea said, frowning against his throat. "At least, I think I do. Didn't you tell me that you loved me, David?"

I've just fallen down the rabbit hole, David thought. "Yes," he said. "I love you. I will love you in six months and in thirty years."

"Will you make love to me again?" She raised her face, and David very willingly began kissing her. "You're not too tired?"

He groaned softly against her mouth. "It's been too bloody long," he said. "I've missed you, Chelsea."

She giggled. "Too long? Have you already forgotten last night, husband?"

"Yes," he said with great honesty. "I guess I have. It's a sign that I can't get enough of you. Come here, you crazy woman."

He pulled the towel away and smiled. She felt so damned good against him. He decided not to think about any consequences that he was certain would eventually plague him to perdition. "I've missed your bottom."

"And I've missed your—" She smiled, closing her fingers around him. "My, my," she said, giving him nipping kisses on his chin, "such enthusiasm! I'm glad you didn't drink as much as I did."

"Never," he said, his hand moving from her bottom to caress her belly. "I love you, Chelsea, and I don't ever want you to forget it."

"Why should I? You're such a gentleman, David. If another drunk woman asks you to marry her in the future, I'll just have to make certain that you're too exhausted to carry through."

He laughed softly against her temple. "Fair enough. Now, wife, let me show you the depths of my enthusiasm."

She quivered at the mental image of him on top of her, deep inside her. "David," she whispered, "I think we'll only be able to *feel* the depths of your enthusiasm."

How, he wondered as he tried to gain a modicum of control, was he not to fall on her and ravish her in a minute flat? It had been so long, so bloody long. He pulled her very inquisitive hand away and pushed her onto her back. "Lie still a moment. I want to see what I've got for the next fifty years."

He lightly held her wrists together above her head. "Very nice," he said, his eyes traveling over her body.

"Very nice, indeed." He lowered his head and gently nipped at her breast. "Warm velvet. Is that what one of your heroes would say?"

"Yes," Chelsea gasped. "With maybe a soft and a pink thrown in."

"And wet?" he asked, his tongue gently lapping over her.

"Probably just damp. Wet sounds almost too explicit, more realistic than romantic."

"Let me check that out," he said. "In a romantic way, of course." He released her wrists, moved on top of her and slid down her body. Her legs parted for him, and he eased comfortably between them, resting his head on her soft belly for a moment. She felt his mouth caressing her scar, what she called her moped memento.

Chelsea felt his marvelous fingers stroking up her thigh and discovered that she was holding her breath. She expelled it when she felt him touching her. "Wet," he said, great satisfaction in his voice. "And soft and inviting and—"

He felt her hands tugging at his hair. "More evidence is needed," he said, and moved down.

Chelsea jerked upward when his warm mouth closed over her. She felt his fingers splayed over her stomach, pressing her back. "And very sweet," he said against her, and she quivered wildly.

She felt his finger ease inside her, felt his mouth warm and demanding, and she cried out. She shouted his name as her legs stiffened. Pleasure crashed through her. Small gasps of feeling continued, and when he entered her, slow and deep, she lifted her hips, tugging at his shoulders.

"David," she said, her voice trembling, "I'm so glad I asked you to marry me. It was the best idea I've ever had in my life." Then she moaned as his fingers slipped between them and found her. "I was so stupid not to grab you by the hair and drag you to my cave when you first asked . . . ah, David . . . me."

"Once again, Chelsea," he said, and she willingly obeyed him.

With great enthusiasm.

"What would a Mark I hero say about that gorgeous, sexy bottom of yours?" he asked some minutes later. He was lying on his back now, and Chelsea was covering him like his own personal blanket.

"Impudent? Sedentary?"

His hands kneaded her buttocks. "Hmmmm," he said. "How about gorgeous and sexy?"

"My heroes would never have to use the same words twice."

"Even when they're close to death from satiation?"

She giggled, raised her face and looked down at him. "You're the gorgeous one, David."

"Are you talking about my bottom? How about soft and white and a marvelous handful?"

"You or me?"

"You, turkey. I'm lean and muscled and virile. And I don't have a bottom. I have hard, sculpted buttocks."

"You read too much," she said, tugging on his earlobe. "Now if you really want to get crazy and euphemistic, how about hard and pulsing and throbbing?"

"Lord, not now, lady. Behold a limp being."

"I'll keep you, limp and everything. David, thank you for marrying me. If I hadn't gotten a tad tipsy I might not have had the courage to ask you."

He refused to think about the century's greatest lie, at least not now, on his ... honeymoon.

"Then why didn't you want to talk to me, Chels? I was the world's most miserable bastard."

She ducked her face down and buried it in the hollow of his neck. "I was scared."

"Of me?"

"Of marriage. And me."

His hands moved again over her bottom. "I need a bit of explanation for that one."

"I'm twenty-eight, David. I was really beginning to think that marriage wasn't for me. And you and I haven't always gotten along, you know."

He chewed that over a bit, then said, "But your heroes and heroines don't get along right away, do they? No, I know they don't. As a member of Chelsea Lattimer's fan club I know for a fact that they fight like wombats and hummingbirds."

"That's ... different. I've always had the niggling suspicion that women tend to equate sexual satisfaction with love. After all, we're not simple like you men are. I was afraid that I was talking myself right into my own theory."

"And what do you think now?" Oddly, he was tense as he asked her that question.

"I think that I'm the luckiest woman alive. If you continue to make love with me, say, twice a day for the next fifty years I probably won't give it much more thought."

"Fair enough," he said. "How many times a night?"

She laughed, hugged him, kissed his chin. "I'm so glad I asked you to marry me!" She arched back and picked up his left hand.

Frowning, she said, "Where's your wedding ring?"

Oh damn! Well, if one had to commit perjury, one might as well do it with panache. "You were in too much of a hurry. Don't you remember? You grabbed this wedding band, then yanked me out of the pawnshop. I think I remember the owner muttering about poor beleaguered men and insatiable women."

"You're lying!"

"Well, maybe just a bit, a tad, a veritable diddling amount."

She kissed him, thoroughly. "This," she said, giving him a very sexy look, "is our honeymoon."

"Yes," he said, his eyes darkening with pleasure, "it most certainly is. Do you want to gamble?"

"You've already won the wager, Dr. Winter!"

"Yes," he said. "Yes, I have, haven't I?"

The consequences of their marriage didn't occur to Chelsea until they were seated cross-legged on the bed, eating a delayed breakfast.

"The children!" she said. "My parents. Your parents. George and Elliot. Cynthia and John. The world."

He chewed on a piece of bacon, gaining great satisfaction from watching the curve of her breasts beneath the pale violet camisole. He managed to pull himself from his fond contemplation. "That sounds like a whole bunch of folks," he said.

"David! No one knows we're married!"

"True enough," he said. He grinned at the thought of Delbert, Angelo and Maurice.

"What will your children think?" She groaned.

"They love you." That was something else to feel guilty about, he thought. "Chelsea," he began slowly, "you do like Mark and Taylor, don't you?"

"Of course I do. It's not me I'm worried about."

"You don't mind being a stepmother to those two little hellions?"

"Not at all. Don't you remember Evangeline, one of my Regency heroines? She adored the hero's little boy, Edward. And don't forget Giana, who became Leah's stepmother."

"Well, that settles it, doesn't it?"

"Yes," she said, smiling, "I suppose it does. As for my parents, they'll be dancing for joy. I can't understand why they thought you, of all men, practically walked on water."

"But they do," David said smoothly. He suddenly paled. "Chels, birth control." He smacked his palm against his forehead. "I'm not using anything and you were . . . well, you were so excited about getting me to the preacher, you didn't use anything, either."

She was silent for a long moment. "We're married, right?"

"Yes," he said, watching her with a fascinated eye.

"Then I can say whatever is in my head, right?"

"Yes," he said again, his fascination growing by leaps and bounds.

"I mean, even if something was embarrassing to me before, now that we're married I shouldn't be reluctant about saying anything I want to?"

"Absolutely."

"All right. I told you I was erratic. Well, I'm not, not usually at any rate. I'm probably due before the end of our honeymoon."

"Bummer," he said.

"Finish your toast, David," she said, wriggling out of her camisole. "Time's awasting."

Chapter 16

It occurred to Chelsea only after she'd fastened her seat belt on the flight from Las Vegas back to San Francisco. "David?"

"Yes, love?"

"How did we get to Las Vegas?"

She wasn't certain, but she thought he flushed just a bit. No, she thought, smiling, that was silly. Perhaps he was just one of those people who were white-knuckled until after the plane was in the air.

"Actually," he said, his brain going into overdrive, "you were so anxious to get me to Nevada and married that I got a friend of mine who owns a private plane to fly us. Don't you remember at all?" Lawyers, he thought, had the right idea about getting themselves off uncomfortable hooks. Ask a question back. Chelsea was looking thoughtful.

"I do remember a loud burring sound and some bumping around. I guess it was the engines of a small plane, huh?"

"Sounds like it was," he said smoothly, and quickly added, "Since we're in first class, we'll get free champagne. You want to indulge in something other than white wine?"

"Fine with me," Chelsea said.

"You know what we can do during the flight?"

She shot him a sexy look, and he shook his head. "Get your one-track mind on different appetites. We need to discuss where we want to go on our real honeymoon."

"Hawaii," she said firmly. "Maui, to be precise. I haven't been there yet."

"You got it. I've never been to Hawaii."

"I go visit Tom Selleck on the tube every week, but it's not exactly the same thing."

"No lusting after other men now, Chelsea."

"I won't have the time or the energy," she said, and accepted a glass of champagne from the flight attendant.

They toasted each other, then David said, "When will you be free, as in between books?"

"In a couple of months. I'm on the last third of the San Francisco trilogy. And guess what, David?"

"Hmm?"

"My hero is a doctor and his nickname is Saint. He's wonderful, needless to say."

"Mark I or Mark II?"

"Definitely Mark II. Well," she added on a wicked grin, "maybe there's a little dash of Mark I in him. But, as I said, he won't be tucked away for about two months yet."

"I'll set up my time, then. Do you have a good travel agency?"

They continued mundane talk, then Chelsea grew silent. David waited a moment, then said, "What's up, honey? You getting post-cold feet?"

She gave him a dazzling smile and shook her head vehemently. "Oh no, husband. I was just thinking about all my writer friends. What Dorothy Garlock, for example, will say about my runaway elopement to Las Vegas is nearly beyond my imagination. Much less Linda Howard and Fayrene Preston and Ann Maxwell—she's Elizabeth Lowell, too, you know—and Laura Parker and Candy Camp and Iris—"

"My God," he said, interrupting her seemingly endless list. "How many phone calls are there going to be?"

"I can't forget my friends Marilyn Staggs and Jean Weisner in Houston. They own bookstores." She moaned. "I think announcements will be the best way to go. I don't think I could take all the verbal abuse I'd get over the phone."

"That's another thing, Chels," he said. "Whose phone?"

She gave him a blank look.

"I mean, where are we going to live?"

"Oh," She looked at him helplessly. "Marriage leads to more consequences than my poor brain can manage."

"My commute from Sausalito to the hospital is only thirty minutes. If you'd feel better about staying at your condo, that's fine with me."

"I love the city, too, and your place." She sat thoughtfully silent for a while, then announced in a firm voice, "I have the most portable profession in the world. All I need is my computer and I'm set. There's no need for you to be driving an hour a day."

"Are you thinking of what we could, ah, accomplish in that hour?"

"You got it," she said, grinning. Her hand roved slowly up his thigh.

He clasped her hand, halting her upward motion. "I can take tomorrow off and we'll move you to the city. All right?"

She nodded, but he could tell she wasn't terribly excited by the prospect.

"Would you like to sell your condo or rent it out?"

"Sell, I guess. Then why don't we buy a house in San Francisco? Maybe an old Victorian in Pacific Heights or Sea Cliff, though I'm not very handy. Are you?"

"No," he said firmly, "not at all handy."

"We'll have to pool our resources and see what we can come up with."

They made the necessary phone calls that evening from David's apartment. It became obvious to Chelsea after her talk with her parents that her dad was disappointed. She said after setting down the receiver, "I've got to think about this." She clasped and unclasped her hands in her lap. "David," she blurted out suddenly, "would you mind if we got married again, for my parents' sake?"

If he could have yelled for joy, he would have. For a moment he simply couldn't believe that she, bless her innocent heart, had suggested the solution to the problem, and so quickly. He'd planned to speak to her parents, as a matter of fact, say in two or three weeks, and have them request another ceremony. He'd dreaded it, just imagining their reaction to what he'd done. He swooped down on her, lifted her bodily off the floor and swung her around. "Do you know how marvelous you are?"

"Well, maybe," she said, looking down into his smiling face. She added, frowning a bit, "You look like a Cheshire cat." That gave him a moment's pause, but her mind was in high gear, and she quickly went on. "There won't be a problem with our marriage license, will there? As in having two of them?"

"Not a single one," he said smoothly, removing that Cheshire cat look, whatever that was.

"And you, you gorgeous man, must have a wedding band. I'm not letting you out of the house without one."

"You're right," he said. "I have to fight the women off all the time. A wedding band might protect me."

"Harrumph," said Chelsea.

"Let's go make love," David said, swinging her up into his arms.

"More controlled experiments for science?"

"You got it, Cookie, although I prefer uncontrolled."

"Let's hear it for science," Chelsea said later, so exhausted she could scarcely move. "I think we can submit this paper now with conclusive proof."

"Proof that women are as easy as men?"

"Proof that you, David Winter, are the sexiest, most talented, neatest...luckiest man on this continent."

"I'll drink to that," David said, and pulled her closer. He said a few moments later in a blurred voice, "Oh, damn, we'd better set the alarm clock. We need to be up and out of here early to get everything done."

Chelsea groaned. "The honeymoon's over."

"Not by a long shot, lady."

"I just wonder how long a shot you're talking about?"

He groaned. "There goes your one-track mind again."

They moved Chelsea the next day in a quickly rented U-Haul. David's apartment looked like a disaster area by the evening. He looked about ruefully. He had believed his place was large and airy.

Chelsea sat down on a packed box. "I can't believe you're going to leave me alone with all this tomorrow."

"Remember your vows. For better and worse." He grinned down at her and ruffled her curly hair. "You'll never walk alone," he said, and made a phone call, arranging for two very strong, healthy young men to arrive in the morning. "All you have to do is supervise, sweetheart."

Chelsea did, with great verve. David came home at about five in the afternoon to a very tidy apartment and a study that was no longer his.

Her computer looked quite at home on *his* antique desk, and the room was lined with bookshelves, filled with her books.

Funny about marriage, he mused. He'd pictured Chelsea in his apartment with great anticipation, but he hadn't quite gotten past that delightful fantasy to the reality of her possessions.

Chelsea saw that he was looking somewhat shell-shocked and said, "I put up temporary shelves in that closet for all your medical journals and books. I'm sorry about being such a space pig, but you work at the hospital and I work at home, and I can't do it in the closet."

"Fair enough," he said with a fond farewell to his formerly very neatly organized things as she shut the closet door.

It did please him inordinately to see her panties next to his shorts in the dresser drawer. He picked up the violet camisole and rubbed it against his cheek. "I shall always have salacious memories about this garment."

"That, David," she said, "is a three-dollar word. I didn't think you doctors were all that well educated."

"I must have read it in one of your books."

She hugged him. "I am so happy," she said, rubbing her nose against his chest, "that I almost hurt. I wish I'd seduced you to Las Vegas a long time ago."

He felt the familiar stab of guilt. "I don't know how much longer I can live with this," he said.

"What?" she asked, looking up at him. "Live with what?"

He looked startled, then realized that he'd spoken aloud. "That is," he said, improvising with quick desperation, "I don't know how much longer I can go without flinging you on the bed."

"Well, I tried my hand at some cooking. Wanna be brave and give it a fling?"

"Before we indulge in our other appetites?"

"Hamburger Happiness," she said. "I don't know what that will lead to, if anything. That reminds me, I've got to talk to Sarah. I'm not at all certain that she'd want to drive to the city all the way from Corte Madera."

"Offer her the moon. If that doesn't work, offer her my poor body."

"Forget that, Champ. Hamburger Happiness. Ugh!"

He grinned at her doleful tone and followed her to the kitchen. She said over her shoulder, on a happier note, "George and Elliot invited us over to dinner tomorrow night. They send their congratulations, by the way."

"Yeah," David said. "I saw Elliot today at the pool. He was grinning from ear to ear." Indeed he was, David thought, feeling that dreadful guilt wash over him again. Delbert, Angelo and Maurice had all called him today, demanding details and chortling like comrades in arms who had just pulled off the most fantastic coup. He added over his third bite of Hamburger Happiness, which wasn't at all bad, "All the folk at the hospital want to give us a party."

"Life isn't going to be simple for a while, is it?"

"What about all your writer friends?"

"I guess I'd best go somewhere and get some announcements. I haven't the foggiest idea of where, though."

"Call George."

"No, I'll call Neff. She'll know. Lord, she lives right here in the city. I'll invite her over and rack her brain."

"Neff who?"

"Well, it's Neff Rotter, also known as Laura Matthews, Elizabeth Neff Walker—"

"How do you guys keep yourselves straight?"

"That, my husband, is a question I should ask you."

He sat back in his chair and crossed his arms over his chest. "I'm beginning to believe that this honeymoon is going to last a good thirty years."

"Well, if I went to all the trouble of getting you to Las Vegas, it better!"

He ducked his head down, feeling a guilty flush wash over his face.

"David?"

"Can I have some more Hamburger Happiness, Chels?"

"Brave, aren't you?"

Yeah, he thought, about as brave as a mushroom.

During the next week, he played over and over in his mind what Chelsea's reaction would be to his confession. No, sweetheart, his mind said, we're not actually married, but we will be soon, or we are now—confession time after the ceremony—so what difference does it make? I did it because I love you and you love me. I just had to get you over your nervousness about it, that's all. You jerk! You made a fool of me! Oh, David it doesn't matter. I love you. You did the right thing. *Damnation!*

Phone calls came in from all over the country from other writers. He happened to pick up the phone one evening and heard, "Is this the gorgeous hunk that finally caught Chelsea?"

"Uh, yes, I guess so," he said to the laughing voice on the other end.

"I can't wait to read her love scenes from now on! You, dear man, are now raw material, buff research."

"Uh, well, let me get Chelsea!" He dropped the phone and sent an agonized look toward his *wife*.

"Hi, Barbara! Is Beth on the other line?" Chelsea asked, and then was silent, a wide grin on her face.

"Yes, oh boy, you're right about that! Yes, that's *moi*! You got it. Thanks for calling."

"Well," Chelsea said, grinning wickedly at him, "you just got your second dose of writer wit. Keenan and Rowe aren't writers but they're close enough— they publish a magazine. Remember Cynthia Wright? She, my dear, was merely your first dose. Hefty, wasn't it?"

"Articulate, to-the-point bunch, aren't you?"

"Yes indeed, but you just wait until Tom Huff finds out. Lordie! Ain't it great?"

He supposed so. His kids had been a bit less artic-ulate, but Mark had asked him quite clearly on the phone if he was kissing Chelsea more now and pat-ting her bottom still. Margaret hadn't been at all sur-prised, and the general sent his best wishes. As for his parents, they'd sent a telegram from the south of France, a very noncommittal telegram.

The only snake in the garden appeared a week and a half later when Chelsea, dancing around when he got home from the hospital, handed him an article from the *Examiner*. It was all about the two of them, and he, the most romantic doctor in the world, had gotten fifty percent of the billing. He continued reading about their whirlwind romance and elopement to Las Vegas. He moaned. "Who," he said, "is responsible for this?"

"I think Barbara called a journalist friend and he called me. What's the matter, David? Don't you like it? There are only a couple of inaccuracies, and they're not anything major."

He said the first thing that popped into his mind, "Hell no! For God's sake, Chelsea, I'm a physician!

This... ridiculous exposè will make my colleagues think I'm nothing more than a—"

"A what, David?"

Menacing tone, he thought, and quickly re-trenched. He managed a deep sigh and said, "Please, in the future, Chels, just ask me, all right?"

"Ask you what? If you feel too above all us ordinary mortals to appear in print? Ask you if it's all right the next time I'm interviewed or on TV to speak about us?"

"No, damn it! Well, maybe. I just feel like I'm on parade, that's all. I don't enjoy feeling like a fool."

"Feeling like a fool because you eloped with me? Feeling like a fool because you married a writer who just happens to write *that* kind of thing? Lord, should I switch to Westerns? How about sci-fi? Ah, mysteries. That's manly, isn't it, with so much more credibility. You wouldn't be so embarrassed and ashamed."

"Stop turning your agile mouth on me, lady!"

"You usually enjoy my agile mouth!"

"I should have said agile tongue!"

"You enjoy that especially!"

"Damn it, keep to the point!"

"There *is* no point, except that I never should have asked you to marry me! You're becoming an uptight Easterner before my very eyes. You didn't even have to go into a phone booth to change into your stuffed shirt!"

"There's no reasoning with you!"

"Yeck!"

And she stomped out, grabbing her purse from the hall stand.

"Chelsea!" he yelled after her. The front door slammed.

He thought suddenly that it was the man who was supposed to slam out. He heard her car rev up and take off, tires screeching.

What, he thought, walking slowly to the window, had the argument been about in the first place? He saw the accursed newspaper article on the floor. Stuffed shirt, was he! Just because he didn't want to appear like some sort of. . . what?

A real life hero?

Marrying a creator of heroes?

Using him for subject matter?

Dumb jerk!

He knew she'd gone back to Sausalito, to her condo. It wasn't rented out yet. What to do? There wasn't any phone service.

He was at the point of driving like a bat out of hell to Sausalito, when the phone rang. It was the hospital, not his "wife." An emergency. He cursed, knowing there was no hope for it, and went in. He was in emergency surgery until two o'clock in the morning.

When he got out of surgery there was a message for him from Chelsea. She was home, *their* home, thank God.

She was asleep when he arrived, for which he was profoundly thankful. He didn't think he was up to apologizing with the proper finesse in his current state of fatigue.

She was still sleeping when he left the next morning. He didn't awaken her. Instead he had red roses delivered.

"It's something a hero would do," she said when he walked in the door that evening. "A hero who feels guilty and doesn't want to talk about it. A Mark I hero who's more macho than sensitive and believes organic matter will save his hide."

"Hi, sweetheart," he said, and pulled her into his arms. He felt so much relief just to have her close to him. "Please, Chelsea, don't walk out on me again. Let's fight until we can't think of any more words, all right? Just don't leave me."

"I didn't mean what I just said. It was awful of me. I'm a dreadful person. You're not a Mark I, except in bed. I'm sorry."

"I love this spate of apologies from both of us," he said, and gently lifted her face. "You're beautiful, I'm proud of you, I'm crazy about you."

"I guess that about covers what I wanted to say, too." She sniffed. It had been a dreadful day, filled with silent pacing, recriminations, a trotting out of all her insecurities.

"Tell you what, love. Let's have a phone booth installed here. Then, if I turn stuffy, you can shove me into it and hand in a starchy white shirt."

"Okay," she said, giving him a wan smile. "And I'll watch my mouth."

"No, let me watch your mouth, or feel your mouth, as the case may be."

"Are we still on our honeymoon, David?"

"I'm not sure. When is the wedding?"

"Next week, at George's house."

"Good, we'll start all over then."

"David?"

"Yes, sweetheart?" He was busily nuzzling her throat.

"The wedding will be very private."

"Hmmm."

"It's the reception."

"Hmmm?"

"It's going to be, well, just a bit larger than antici-
pated."

He drew back and looked down into her beloved
face, which expressed guilt and wariness. "No," he
said softly, placing a fingertip over her lips. "Don't tell
me. I don't want to know. All I want right now is for
you to make love with me."

She felt that marvelous warmth curling through her.
"How can I turn down an offer like that?"

"You can't," he said, tossing her, laughing, over his
shoulder and patting the most beautiful bottom in the
world.

Chapter 17

David couldn't believe it. He stared down at the pair of leopard-print underwear and the funny note that accompanied it. He might have known. It was from Cynthia and John-blond-haired-Sanchez who had tried to kill his dog with a rake. George peered over his shoulder, burst into laughter, grabbed the appalling wedding present out of his hands and tossed it to an emergency room nurse.

David managed to slither out of the living room under cover of the roars of laughter from the guests. He continued slithering like a shadow against the wall until he found the safety of the Mallorys' kitchen. It was filled to bursting with people chopping and cooking, and people hefting up trays of food to serve the guests. He found the back door and kept slithering until he reached an isolated part of their small garden.

He sat down on the lone stone bench and leaned back, closing his eyes. You're about ready for the phone booth, he told himself. So what's the big deal about a pair of leopard jockey shorts? A good half the presents they'd received were gag gifts. Lord, he just wanted it all to be over with, all resolved, he and Chelsea finally married—for the second time, of course.

It was nice of the Mallorys to have gone to so much trouble—this party followed by the wedding and the reception afterward. Just three more days, he told himself.

Tomorrow he and Chelsea would go out and buy him a wedding ring, and, he'd insisted, an engagement ring for her. He suddenly remembered the engagement parties and the wedding reception he and Margaret had been given. They had, he decided, perking up, been very formal, very tasteful and very boring. He remembered now that he'd never seen so much silver in his life. He wondered what had happened to all those teapots and serving trays.

"Hi. What's up, Doc?"

He looked up to see Chelsea smiling down at him. "I was just counting my blessings," he said, then added, grinning, "and my leopard shorts."

"You feeling overwhelmed?" Chelsea asked, having seen him slink out of the living room.

He patted the bench beside him, and she eased down. "I love you," he said, and pulled her into his arms. "And I wish we were alone, doing crazy, wonderful things to each other."

"That's a plan I second," Chelsea said, and leaned against his shoulder, sighing. "Everyone is so kind and so much fun, and really, so marvelous—"

"But?"

"I just wish this were the wedding reception and that would spell the end of all the festivities."

"I do like that sexy nightwear you got, though. Who was that from?"

"I honestly don't remember," she said.

"Well, I think that sinful red cutout nightgown will spell the beginning of our festivities."

She giggled, feeling suddenly relaxed for the first time in days. The novel was going exceedingly slowly. Her doctor hero Saint was definitely taking a back seat to her doctor hero David. There was just so much to do, so much to occupy her mind. She ran her hand over his chest. "All mine," she said.

"Yes, ma'am. You've got a fifty-year lease on this property."

"Is there oil in these here hills?"

David was feeling punch-drunk and couldn't think of a retort. Her mind never slowed down, never. Well, maybe when she was in bed with him. He seemed now to recall once when he'd had the last word. She'd just lain there, staring up at him with blurred, vague eyes, a silly smile on her face.

"Three more days to go, sweetheart, then we'll hole up. Okay?"

She nodded against his shoulder.

"When are your parents coming in?"

"Tomorrow." She gave a shudder. "I can't imagine what they're going to give us for a wedding present."

"Let me shudder with you."

Actually, the Lattimers' wedding present, presented the following evening at their apartment, was their trip to Hawaii, including the honeymoon suite at Kapalua Bay and a Mercedes to drive around the island. It was an incredibly generous gift.

"What do you think, Cookie?"

"Oh, Dad!" Chelsea threw her arms around her father, kissed him soundly, then dove for her mother. "You guys are too much!"

Mimi Lattimer gave her daughter a fond, teary look and pressed a long, narrow box into her hands. "Just a little something for you, dear."

Chelsea shot a look at David, then opened the wrapping and the jeweler's box. Inside was a diamond-and-emerald necklace, exquisitely fashioned. Chelsea simply stared at it. Then she looked up at David and burst into tears.

"Cookie!"

"Lovey!"

"It's so beautiful," Chelsea sobbed against David's chest.

"It is, indeed," David said, smiling at Chelsea's parents over her head. "Come on, sweetheart, you're going to take all the starch out of my white shirt."

He stroked her hair for a moment, then said, "I'd like a drink. How about you guys?"

"A margarita," said Mimi.

"White wine, like my little girl. Come on, Cookie, we couldn't give you gold. You might outshine your old man."

David grinned ruefully as Harold Lattimer ran his fingers over his gold necklace.

"First," David said, "I want to see Chelsea in the necklace. Go blow your nose, sweetheart, then get back here."

The necklace looked exquisite, and David took back every snobbish thought he'd ever entertained about her parents. He wished suddenly that his own parents could show their love so openly and warmly.

After the Lattimers left for the evening David took himself off to the shower. Chelsea went to the other bathroom and took off the incredible necklace. "Well," she told her image in the mirror, "if you ever run out of ideas, you won't starve for at least six months." She lovingly laid the necklace back in its box. Her gold band caught on the clasp and she gasped, terrified that she'd hurt the necklace. Slowly, carefully, she pulled the clasp free of the ring, and in the process scratched her wedding band.

"Oh, no," she wailed. For the first time she tugged off her ring and examined it under the light. Just a very slight scratch. She held it in her palm for a moment, wondering suddenly what woman had sold the ring. She hadn't felt at all strange about wearing another woman's wedding ring until now. Had she been an obsessive gambler? How sad if it were true. She held the ring up to the light again, closely examining the inside of the band. She realized that it was old, very old. She squinted.

There was writing. She rubbed the inside with a tissue and looked again.

She froze.

David was tired when he emerged from the shower, but not that tired, and he was surprised and disappointed to see Chelsea curled up on her side, her back to him, sound asleep.

He didn't wake her. She must be exhausted. He quietly got into bed beside her and turned off the bedside lamp. He lay on his back, his head pillowed on his arms, and stared up at the dark ceiling. Day after tomorrow and it would all be over. Of course, that thought led to his inevitable confession. He groaned to himself. He should be up for the Chicken of the Year award. What the hell should he do now? What if he told her before the wedding and she freaked out and told him to go to hell? What if she just looked at him, her wonderful, expressive eyes wounded? Would she ever trust him again? What if? What if? He was making himself crazy. He couldn't go on like this. He had to come clean.

"No, David. No way. Just forget it."

"I can't, Elliot," David said miserably. "I love her, and what I did was—"

"What you did was give Chelsea what she wanted," Elliot said, interrupting him firmly. "Besides, it's a little late, isn't it? The wedding's tomorrow."

David cursed.

"Hasn't she been saying continuously that she wished she'd asked you to marry her sooner? Isn't she happy as a pie-eyed clam? Doesn't she love you to distraction?"

"Yes and yes and yes, but—"

"Fine, tell her, or better yet, go talk to her parents."

"You think it would be a good idea? Get their opinion and all that? What if they look at me like I'm some sort of fiend straight up from Hades?"

Elliot studied his friend closely. David was suffering, and here Elliot was being glib and a know-it-all. David felt guilty, and Elliot didn't blame him, but it *had* seemed the best thing to do at the time. They were all guilty, guilty as hell. But what to do? He couldn't begin to imagine Chelsea's reaction if David confessed prior to the wedding. She would laugh and forgive him—that's what she'd do. At least it sounded good, he thought. Elliot sighed. Why wasn't life ever simple?

The matter was taken out of David's hands. The night before their wedding Chelsea's parents insisted she stay at the Fairmont with them. Chelsea, who had agreed to her parents' request with more enthusiasm than he liked, smiled up at him and gave him a subdued goodbye kiss. He thought indulgently that she had a super case of nerves. In all honesty, though, he was feeling subdued himself.

He spent a lonely night in the empty expanse of the bed. It was nearly two o'clock in the morning when he made his decision. He would tell her on their honeymoon. He felt like an Atlas who no longer carried the world on his shoulders.

The wedding, at the Mallorys' house, was as private as David and Chelsea wanted, and it went quite smoothly, with only the Mallorys and Chelsea's parents present. Chelsea, to David's chagrin, whispered to him after the Reverend MacPherson had pronounced them husband and wife, "Did our ceremony in Las Vegas go as quickly?"

"I don't remember," David said, his stomach curdling.

She looked so perfect, he thought, dressed in a soft cream silk dress, the beautiful necklace at her throat. She was now wearing both an engagement ring and her wedding band.

They had an hour before the reception to unwind a bit. George, a bird of such glorious plumage that it almost hurt to look at her, sidled up to her husband and whispered, "'All's well that ends well,' I've decided."

"Yes," Elliot said. "Yes, indeed. And Alex kept decently quiet through the whole thing."

"A perfect child," George said.

"I'd best go upstairs and see if his nurse had to gag him."

George crossed the living room to hug Chelsea. She watched her friend for a moment. Chelsea was holding her marriage license. The expression on her face made George frown a bit. It was an odd look. She tried to remember if she had stared with a bemused expression at her own marriage license. She didn't think she had.

Well, no accounting for people's reactions. She heard her small son's lusty cries from upstairs and grinned. He probably had been gagged during the ceremony.

"Every time I marry you I buckle up," Chelsea said, fastening her seat belt on the plane that would take them directly to Maui.

"Ah, yes, it seems so," David said.

They were silent until the plane was in the air.

"You happy, sweetheart?"

She turned to face him, and he felt himself melt. "You're so very beautiful," he said, and kissed her. They separated at a slight cough from the flight attendant.

"Honeymooners?"

"Yes," they said together.

"Well, a present was sent on board for you." The woman lifted a bottle of Dom Perignon for their inspection, a huge red bow around its neck.

"From my publisher," Chelsea said, carefully pulling away the card from the bow. "Just look at this list of names, David!"

He did and was impressed. He was married to a very successful woman, and it pleased him inordinately. It occurred to him that even a year ago he would probably have been threatened by his wife's independent success. No, he corrected himself, he would never have been such a stuffed shirt as all that.

"Will you support me in the manner to which I'm accustomed?" he asked as the flight attendant poured them two glasses of the champagne.

"Well," Chelsea said quite seriously as she toasted him, "my income has steadily increased with each contract. Who knows? Maybe in five years you'll be eating bonbons on the beach, giving lewd looks to underage girls in scanty bikinis."

"Now that sounds like a plan," he said, and felt the champagne bubbles tickle his nose as he drank.

The flight passed pleasantly, and they weren't too conked out by the time they reached the Kapalua Bay

Hotel on Maui. The drive from the airport took a good hour, but the scenery was beautiful, and David, who had never been to paradise before, was duly impressed.

They spent the rest of the afternoon in bed, emerging only at seven in the evening for dinner. A walk on the beach in the moonlight, David was thinking. Tonight was D-Day. Or D-Night, as it were.

Yes, he repeated grimly to himself as he forked down a delicious bite of lobster, tonight it would be. He watched his wife down two glasses of white wine. I'm a cunning, devious bastard, he thought as he offered her another.

Chelsea slipped off her panty hose behind a tree and stuffed them into one of her shoes. It was idyllic. Moonlight, the crashing ocean waves, the balmy evening.

"Chelsea," David said finally, the word barely emerging from his tight throat.

"Yes, love?"

Dreamy voice, he thought. Onward. "There's something I need to tell you."

She stopped a moment and turned to face him. She had a sweet smile on her face. "Yes?"

He loosened his tie. "It's about Las Vegas."

"Yes?"

More interest in her voice now. But still dreamy.

"Well, you remember how we were playing poker that evening with Delbert, Maurice and Angelo?"

"How could I forget? I lost over fifty bucks."

Voice smooth, unsuspecting—loving, in fact.

He blurted out, "I slipped you a Mickey!"

She didn't say a word, merely stared up at him, her shoes dangling in her hand.

"Well, actually, it was one of the guys who slipped it in your glass. Then you spilled the wine and we did it again."

"Hmmm," she said. "So that's what made my mouth feel like a drought had hit."

He stared at her, not believing her calm, matter-of-fact voice.

"Chelsea," he said, his voice desperate now, his confession almost finished, "we really didn't get married in Las Vegas. I lied to you. I wanted you so much and I knew you wanted me and so . . . well, I did it."

Silence.

She said, very softly, "Did you regret doing it, David? Pretending to marry me, I mean."

"God, no! But I've felt so guilty, like a damned worm. I was too chicken to tell you sooner."

The moonlight fell over his face, and the gentle breeze ruffled his hair. She slowly raised her hand and smoothed it back from his forehead.

"Say something, damn it!"

"All right," she said agreeably. "I know."

"Know what?" he said, stiffening.

"A lot of things, actually," Chelsea said, teasing him just a bit.

"Chelsea—"

"Here, David, hold this for a minute."

He watched silently as she slipped off her engagement ring. He took it from her, feeling edgy, wary and bewildered.

She worked off the wedding band and held it up in the moonlight. "I don't think you can see anything out here. The light isn't bright enough, but I'll tell you. There's an inscription inside the ring. It says, *Rebecca Winter, 1915*. Your grandmother, David?"

"Yes," he said. "I loved her very much."

Another couple strolled past them, hand in hand.

"When did you find out?" he asked finally.

"Does it matter?" she said, a small smile playing about her mouth.

"You don't want to send me to the castration center in Sacramento?"

"Perhaps, but for just a little while. It was a marvelous Mark I thing to do, I decided. Forgive me for letting you suffer, but I thought you deserved it for just a little while."

"You wouldn't have said anything?"

"Not until you did."

"I was thinking at one point that I'd wait until our tenth wedding anniversary."

"Then," Chelsea said in a serene voice, "that's when I would have said something. Who knows? Maybe our kids would have overheard."

"Put the ring back on, Chelsea."

She did, then the engagement ring.

He pulled her into his arms. "Is this as romantic as one of your novels?"

"More so," Chelsea said, pulling his head down so she could kiss him. "This is real."

"You truly forgive me for what I did?" he said, nuzzling his mouth against her hair.

"I'll probably use it in a novel," she said. "Now, David, how's your energy level?"

"You want a moonlight swim?"

"That's a start, I suppose."

"What would a Mark I hero do?"

"You tell me, and that will go in the novel, too," she said, and leaned back in the circle of his arms, waiting for him to speak.

"I guess I'm feeling so happy and so sinfully relieved that I'll just have to sit here on the beach and contemplate my incredible good fortune."

She laughed.

David said, "Have I had the last word for once?"

"Don't hold your breath, Doctor," Chelsea said, and wrapped herself around him.

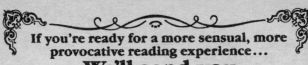

COMING NEXT MONTH

#193 KISS OF THE DRAGON—Barbara Faith

Her dying father's request brought Bethany Adams to Hong Kong. There, Tiger Malone swept Bethany up in a hunt through China, where they risked their lives to find a golden dragon and discovered a greater treasure—love.

#194 LEGACY—Maura Seger

Gwen Llywelyn came to Wales to see her ancestral home, but she found much more: mysterious tremors and power failures—and Owen Garrett. Owen wasn't exactly who he said he was, but Gwen quickly decided he was all she'd ever wanted.

#195 THE GENUINE ARTICLE—
Katheryn Brett

A. J. McMichaels expected life in her small hometown to be uneventful, not sizzling with rumors of political corruption. She didn't expect to find herself feuding with the mayor, Rich Beckman, either—and she certainly didn't expect to fall in love with him.

#196 GYPSY DANCER—Kathleen Creighton

For Lily Fazekas, going to Hungary was a romantic quest for the family she had never known. Joseph Varga's assignment was to stay with her until the search was over, but long before that time arrived, he knew he wanted to stay with her—forever.

AVAILABLE THIS MONTH:

GILLIAN HALL

The magnificent novel of a woman
fighting for her greatest passion—
and for a love to fulfill
her deepest desires.

The desire to break from an unbearable past takes prima ballerina
Anna Duras to Broadway, in search of the happiness she once knew.
The tumultuous changes that follow lead her to the triumph of new
success . . . and the promise of her greatest love.

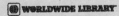